## "Don't yell, sugar."

Garth practically fell on her to put a hand over her mouth. "It's me."

Deedee said something against his palm, but the pressure of his hand made it unintelligible.

"This isn't what it looks like, sugar," he whispered. "I was returning your ferret. She got into my room." He tried to sound reasonable and unthreatening.

She stared at him. The alarm in her eyes had diminished, but wasn't totally gone. "If you promise to be calm, I'll take my hand away."

When he sat back, she narrowed her eyes to slits and glared at him. "You don't expect me to *believe* that story, do you?" She lay there, stiff, her body language telling him she trusted him about as far as she could toss a horse.

He shrugged. "Come on, sugar. Give me points for originality, at least."

"That's what I thought!" She sat up, and her glance flicked to his bare chest. Her eyes grew wide.

He shook his head. "I'm wearing shorts." He winked. "Don't want to make it too easy for you."

Dear Reader,

Runaway brides and runaways seem to be the theme this month in a pair of great romps!

Renee Roszel always writes great comedy about heroes and heroines you really do fall in love with, and *There Goes the Bride* (rather self-explanatory) is no different. It is also the first of a mini marathon of Western-themed romances coming out in the next four months. Cowboys and the women who lasso their hearts. You, too, will fall head over spurs for these love stories!

Cheryl Anne Porter's heroine can think of only one really safe place to hide from the Mafia, and therefore confesses to a crime she didn't commit. The only problem is that no one thinks she's guilty—certainly not the sexy deputy assigned to escort her to jail. The only thing to do is to plan *The Great Escape*.

So take some time to smell the roses (it is May!) and enjoy yourself with two great LOVE & LAUGHTER books.

*Malle Vallik*

Malle Vallik
Associate Senior Editor

# THERE GOES THE BRIDE
## Renee Roszel

## *Harlequin Books*

TORONTO • NEW YORK • LONDON
AMSTERDAM • PARIS • SYDNEY • HAMBURG
STOCKHOLM • ATHENS • TOKYO • MILAN
MADRID • WARSAW • BUDAPEST • AUCKLAND

If you purchased this book without a cover you should be aware that this book is stolen property. It was reported as "unsold and destroyed" to the publisher, and neither the author nor the publisher has received any payment for this "stripped book."

ISBN 0-373-44043-X

THERE GOES THE BRIDE

Copyright © 1998 by Renee Roszel Wilson

All rights reserved. Except for use in any review, the reproduction or utilization of this work in whole or in part in any form by any electronic, mechanical or other means, now known or hereafter invented, including xerography, photocopying and recording, or in any information storage or retrieval system, is forbidden without the written permission of the publisher, Harlequin Enterprises Limited, 225 Duncan Mill Road, Don Mills, Ontario, Canada M3B 3K9.

All characters in this book have no existence outside the imagination of the author and have no relation whatsoever to anyone bearing the same name or names. They are not even distantly inspired by any individual known or unknown to the author, and all incidents are pure invention.

This edition published by arrangement with Harlequin Books S.A.

® and TM are trademarks of the publisher. Trademarks indicated with ® are registered in the United States Patent and Trademark Office, the Canadian Trade Marks Office and in other countries.

**Printed in U.S.A.**

# Author Bio

One thing Renee Roszel loves most about writing romance is the friendly folk she meets along the way. She admits she didn't know a thing about saddle making before she started *There Goes the Bride,* so she was a little nervous when she decided to drop in on Mock Brothers' Saddlery near Tulsa.

She ventured back to the saddle-making area with fear and trepidation. Would these rough-and-tumble cowboy types offer to help her research her hero's profession, or would they laugh at her and send her on her "silly romance writer's way"? Well, much to her delight, Renee found herself welcomed by Greg Mock, a most charming and thoroughly gentlemanly cowboy. Wearing his black Stetson, crisp Western shirt, silver belt buckle, slim-fitting jeans and boots—not to mention the sexiest mustache Renee can recall seeing—he escorted her around a workshop redolent with the masculine scent of tanned leather. Her questions were answered with a lot of "Yes, ma'am"s and "No, ma'am"s and irresistible grins. Even her nuttiest questions were answered—like, "If the heroine wants to throw a hammer at the hero, which would be the heaviest?" With an amused quirk of a nice pair of male lips, even that question got answered. Don'tcha just *love* cowboys?

Renee insists—with her tongue planted firmly in her cheek—that research is grueling, thankless work, but she assures us she's willing to make the sacrifice for her readers.

And speaking of readers, Renee loves to hear from them. Write to her at P.O. Box 700154, Tulsa, OK 74170.

I am the Wizard!
Do not look behind the curtain or you will see
Sonnie, Michele, Sally, Hillary, Leslie, Amy,
Donna and Dick
operating the levers behind the scenes.
Thanks, guys!

# 1

MOVEMENT CAUGHT Garth's attention. He looked out the pickup's side window, then squinted, not sure he was seeing right. A woman in a flowing wedding gown barreled down the wide steps of one of Tulsa's most palatial churches. His first thought was that a wedding was just ending, but there was something wrong with the picture. This bride was alone. Garth wasn't a big expert on weddings, but he figured the happy couple usually left together.

Followed by a mile of lacy train, the woman sprinted across the sidewalk and vaulted into the street, heading directly for his truck. Wagging her bouquet wildly, she yelled something.

Never one to ignore a damsel in distress, he rolled down his window. Hot June air rushed into the air-conditioned cab, but he had only a split second to register the weather before he was hit in the face by a salad of roses.

"What the *mffrrup?*" He felt gut-punched, then went blind when a sea of white flooded over him.

He heard a female shriek, "Step on it!"

Spitting greenery, he batted away the fog of lace. "Lady, I don't take orders from insane people." He shoved the heap of fabric aside and glared at the tidal wave of female dry goods that had slithered through his pickup's window.

The bride was watching him through round, rimless glasses. Her blue eyes wide, her lips parted, she panted to catch her breath. Except for the wedding dress—and the fact that she'd dived through his window—she didn't *look* crazy. She didn't look much like a carjacker, either, but if she was one, he had a feeling he could take her.

The situation was suddenly so preposterous he couldn't hold back a grin. "I've had this fantasy, sugar." He scanned the mound of lacy material that hid her from the neck down. "Except in my version you were wearing only a veil, a garter belt and six-inch heels."

She didn't seem to register his joke. Flushed and pre-occupied, she bent forward to look out his window. Those big eyes grew huge and round. "Oh—hurry! They're coming!"

Garth glanced toward the church. Several tuxedoed men rushed out of the cathedral's arched entryway. At the same time a low-pitched honk behind made it clear the light had turned green. The woman at his side made a guttural sound of panic. "Go!" she cried. *"Please!"*

As he rolled up his window, several more get-your-tail-in-gear honks filled the muggy air, mingling with a chorus of salty words ringing from the church steps. The noise became a surreal concert—the Grand Ole' Opry from hell. Without analyzing the right or wrong of it, Garth stepped on the gas. For some reason those panicked blue eyes gave him all the reason he needed. Even pulling a horse trailer full of horse, he managed to make a fair getaway.

As the pickup burned rubber, a tall blond man in a tux almost caught up with them. Through the sideview mirror Garth watched the guy take a mighty leap and just miss the trailer's tailgate. When he stumbled to a halt, the expensively clad man hunched over, panting. As a parting gesture, he flipped them a one-finger salute.

Garth frowned. The preppie jerk looked familiar. Though Garth's mood was already in the crapper, he decided not to pull over and beat the tar out of the penguin. If that was the groom, he probably had a right to be a little hacked off. Besides, this damn detour had already caused Garth more trouble than he needed. He only hoped the little commando-in-bride's-clothing hadn't stolen the church's poor box and made a run for it.

He glanced at her. "Tell me this isn't going to get me on *America's Most Wanted.*"

She twisted around, craning her neck to look behind. "I think we've lost them." Facing him, she eased back into the passenger seat. "I didn't do anything wrong, if that's what you're worried about."

He peered at her. "Lady, right now my main worry is my dog. I hope to hell you didn't kill him." With one hand on the wheel, he fished under the lacy fabric. "You alive in there, boy?"

No sound emerged.

"Oh, no!" the woman cried. "I didn't kill anything, did I?"

"The report's still out on my spleen," he groused, feeling around until his hand hit warm, living tissue. "Dawg?" He palmed something, but it was softer and smoother than his dog had ever felt on his softest, smoothest day.

"Hey, that's me!" The woman slapped at his hand through the fabric.

Garth eyed her askance. "Sorry." Hell. The woman *was* wearing a garter belt. He shifted, readjusting jeans that had become uncomfortably binding. "Dawg?" He gritted his teeth. "Give me a break. If you're not dead, show yourself."

There was movement under a mass of lace near his leg. After a few seconds, a shaggy gray head worked its way out. Garth grinned at the furry imitation of a doormat. "You move pretty fast when you need to, don't you, boy." He shoved at the wedding gown. "Come on up here."

The mutt clambered onto the dress. "Ouch!" The woman grabbed at her hair. "He's sitting on the train."

"Hell, sugar, half the county could ride that train and you'd still have room to haul a load of cow patties."

She winced, her head caught sideways by the dog's weight on her voluminous veil. "What are you?" She grunted, tugging at the lace. "Some kind of cowboy?"

His lips quirked at her disgusted tone. She'd said it like she'd run smack-dab into a revenue agent. "What gave me away, sugar?" he drawled. "Or do all your investment-banker friends pull horse trailers?"

Her hands fluttered to her head, and after she'd removed a few clips, the flowered crown fell away. "I guess beggars can't be choosers," she muttered, brushing off the head-piece as though it was a stray leaf.

"You're welcome," Garth said mockingly. "Anytime."

She shook out her short brown hair and looked at him, her expression contrite. "Sorry. I didn't mean to insult you. It's just that—well, let's say I left the ranch a long time ago, that's all."

Garth watched the road for detour signs. In a few minutes he would be able to get back onto Highway 244. "Look, lady, I'm heading out east of town. Where do you want me to drop you? Maybe Vinita? I hear the state mental hospital there has a real nice bridal suite."

Running both hands through her hair, she twisted in the seat to see him better. "You think I'm crazy?"

He gave her a thorough once-over, lifting one brow. "Hell, sugar, I'm no doctor. But speaking as the man you just force-fed a handful of rose petals, I can't rightly vote for normal."

Her lower lip began to tremble and she bit it, too late to hide her emotional state.

He felt a stab of compassion, but didn't know what to

say. Turning onto the highway access road, he frowned, having had a sudden flash of insight. "I know where I've seen that guy before. In the papers." He glanced her way. "The blond penguin was Tyler DeWinter."

She nodded, but avoided his eyes.

"Doesn't his family own the Tulsa *American-Gazette*, and some other property around here?"

She sighed, pushing her glasses up the bridge of her nose. "The DeWinter Mall, the DeWinter Medical Plaza, DeWinter Pipeline..." she recited in a dismal monotone. "And there's the DeWinter Savings and Loan, the De-Winter Arms and a couple of other residential buildings." She picked at a thread in her gown. "I live—rather, I lived in one of their apartment complexes. And I work at their newspaper."

"You ran out on the DeWinter millions?" Garth whistled long and low, watching her as she self-consciously fingered a rip in her dress.

She nodded. "Right in the middle of our wedding, I ran out on Tyler Maximilian DeWinter IV."

As Garth wove into highway traffic, he found himself at a loss for words, something that didn't happen often. He glanced at her, feeling another tug of pity. Counseling runaway brides wasn't his area of expertise. One or two had picked him to be their rebound lover, and he'd obliged, but he had a feeling this little bird wasn't in the market for cheap sex. She looked more like the type to console herself with a bowl of chocolate ice cream and a romance novel.

He turned away. After a minute, he felt her watching him. He pictured her blue eyes, wide and frightened. When he peered at her, she nervously readjusted her glasses. "I—I guess I screwed up any chance of going back to my job. And with all the clout the DeWinter family has, I'll have a hard time finding another job—or another apartment.''

Garth frowned. ''You sound screwed to me, sugar. Do you have family anyplace?''

''No...no, I'm alone.'' She bit her lower lip and spun to look out her window. Garth had a gut feeling she was getting ready to bawl. ''You want a handkerchief?''

She shook her head and sniffed.

*Women!* Blowing a breath out through clenched teeth, he shifted to retrieve a crumpled red bandanna from his back pocket. ''Here.'' He nudged her arm. ''On the house.''

Without looking, she grabbed the neckerchief and put it to noisy use. ''Thanks,'' she whispered.

She looked so little and lost hunched there, her forehead pressed against the window. He didn't know what in blazes to do, but he felt like he should try something. ''It's none of my business,'' he began, testing the idea aloud, ''but what if you went back and told DeWinter your dosage was off today, or something?''

''My *dosage?*'' Dabbing at her eyes, she gaped at him. ''What kind of salad-munching, pill-popping neurotic do you think I am?''

''Hold on, sugar. Did I ever mention the word *salad?*'' He grinned, trying to lighten the mood.

She glowered at him, but after a few seconds, her expression eased to merely sad. ''This isn't funny. My life's a mess.'' She sagged against the door, closing her eyes. ''I can't go back. I wouldn't if I could. The truth is, I don't love Ty.'' She sat up and pinned Garth with a flinty stare. ''Why else would I run away?''

He shrugged, working to keep his attention on the road. ''If you don't love the guy, then you did the right thing.'' He met her gaze for a second. ''Can't give you points for timing, though.''

She visibly sagged. "That was bad, I know." Wiping her eyes with the bandanna, she murmured, "It all happened so fast. I was standing there, listening to the minister say something about for better or for worse, and it hit me—I didn't want Tyler 'for worse'. That instant I knew I'd let the DeWinter money blind me. And—and suddenly I was running."

He pursed his lips in thought. "Okay, so you get points for integrity." He looked at her. "Too bad it doesn't get you a place to live or a job."

She pressed her hands to her temples as though a headache was coming on. "Don't go into the inspirational speaking business," she moaned. "You'd flop."

"Sorry." He made an apologetic face. "I'm getting near my turnoff. Where do you want to go?"

He glanced at her as she dropped her gaze to her fidgeting hands. Reluctantly he turned back to scan the highway. She said nothing for such a long time he cast her a worried look. She was dragging a diamond ring off her finger. Garth didn't know or care much about jewels, but figured that rock could choke a calf. "What are you doing?"

She started to roll down the window. Sensing what she was about to do, he grabbed her fist. "Whoa, sugar. Let's not be hasty. I didn't see a purse tumble through the window with you. You may need that."

She looked at him, her eyes wet with tears. "Oh—of course. I guess that was a crazy idea." She sniffed, shaking her head. "But I can't keep it. This mess wasn't Ty's fault." She slid the ring into Garth's hand. "You hold it for me until I can find a way to return it, okay?"

Startled, he wrapped his fingers around the ring, his glance lifting to the flow of traffic. "I realize you're not in your right mind, but handing over a rock like this to a stranger isn't very bright.''

He heard her sigh. "You won't steal it."

"How in thunder do you know that?"

Her glistening eyes met his. "The same way I knew you'd help me." A tear slid down her cheek, but she managed a quivering smile. "You have an honest profile."

"An honest profile?" he repeated, incredulous. "Right."

He heard her blow into the bandanna again, but she didn't respond.

After a tense silence, he lifted the ring to inspect the gigantic square diamond. "I'm thinking this isn't one of those cubic zucchini fakes, right?"

She made a halfhearted chuckling sound at his joke. "It's a DeWinter heirloom. Ty said it's worth seventy-five thousand."

Garth whistled. "I've changed my mind." Leaning toward her, he opened the glove box and tossed the ring inside. "I'm giving you a whole passel of integrity points. I know women who'd marry a pile of puke for that ring."

"Thanks, cowboy." Though he was watching the highway, he could see her run her hands through her hair. "What's this town coming up here? Catoosa?"

"Yeah. My grandparents have a little spread not far from here. It's Grandpa's birthday and I'm damn late."

"Oh." The word sounded so pitiful he felt like smacking something. But he didn't figure bruising his knuckles would help her situation much. "If you could drop me off on the main street, I'll be okay."

He pictured that in his mind and a rock formed in his stomach. He was getting his second gut feeling today, and it wasn't good. Why couldn't he let well enough alone—drop her off and be on his way? "What do you think you're going to do on the main street of Catoosa with no clothes and no money?''

Though he didn't turn to look at her, he could tell she was staring out her window, probably trying to hide another bout of tears. "I—I..."

When she didn't say anything else, he spent five minutes telling himself to mind his own business. Finally, strangling the wheel, he pulled over to the shoulder of the highway and stopped. "Sounds like a mighty good plan, sugar. Thanks for sharing.''

She twisted around, looking tragic and confused. "What?''

He eyed her narrowly. "Didn't you just explain to me in great detail how you figure to get clothes, food and lodging in Catoosa?'' Settling a forearm along the top of his steering wheel, he leaned toward her. "Look, sugar, where's your bank?'' he asked more sympathetically. "Maybe I could—''

"My savings went into this.'' She clutched a handful of her gown and held it up. "I'm not your problem. Besides, you said you're late. Drop me off anyplace in town.''

"Fine.'' His sage nod reeked with sarcasm. "In a couple of hours it'll be dark. You can stand on some corner, wave at boozy no-necks cruising for a good time. Call yourself the Hooker Bride. You'll make out real fine.''

She visibly paled and Garth felt like he'd thrown a kitten into a raging river. After blinking several times, she lifted her chin in a poignant show of bravery—or naive foolhardiness. "Just drive, okay?''

Impatient with her I'm-determined-to-burn-at-the-stake attitude, he shifted into gear and pulled back onto the highway. In another minute they'd be at the Catoosa exit. "You can't even sell the damn dress. It's torn.''

"I know.''

He eyed her for a second. She was staring straight ahead, Little Miss Martyrdom. "Look," he said sternly, "running out on your wedding is not a sin." His own past experience with marriage flooded back and he winced. "Don't damn yourself to hell for it."

"I'm not."

"Yeah, right." He felt a rush of frustration. "What do you think you'll do when I let you out—wander around looking for *more* honest profiles?"

"Why not?" She met his gaze, but couldn't hold it. "There are lots of good people in the world."

"And lots of slime, too, sugar."

She spun to face him. "What's your point? Are *you* going to take me in?"

He flashed her a dark look, feeling like crap. He could think of five million reasons why it wouldn't be a good idea to take her in. Most of them were tangled up with sex. He didn't seem to be able to have platonic female friends. He'd tried, dang it, but it never worked. She'd end up in his bed, rebounding her brains out. He had a sixth sense when it came to women. And right now it was telling him she wasn't the type to take well to no-strings fun and games. He didn't want to be responsible for messing up her mind any more than it already was. "Look, sugar, I don't think staying with me would—"

"*Fine,*" she interrupted. "Then don't lecture me."

Twisting to face the front, she went stiff, looking resolved to throw herself to the first wolf who presented her with her idea of an honest profile. *Heaven help the terminally naive.* He mouthed a curse. "What kind of work do you do?"

"I write—or rather, *wrote*—the 'Helpful Winnie's Household Hints' column for the *American-Gazette.*"

"I doubt if Catoosa has many openings for household-hints columnists."

"I've learned a lot from writing that column. I can clean anything—you'd be amazed what a little toothpaste can do."

"That so?" He glanced her way, fighting an urge to tell her a few lewd things he'd done with toothpaste over the years. Maybe now wasn't the best time to taint this kitten-woman's lofty opinion of the product. Without further comment, he turned back to concentrate on the road.

The Catoosa exit came—and went. He could sense her baffled stare. "What—what are you doing?"

He looked at her and was met with a whimsical sight—a Bizarro cartoon of a two-headed freak bride. One head had a rather cute flushed face, curly brown hair and blue eyes, made gigantic by spectacles. The other head was dusty and shaggy gray, with rheumy black eyes. Lolling out of its snaggle-toothed mouth was a long, wet tongue, dribbling on crushed lace.

Shaking his head, Garth turned away, muttering, "I don't throw kittens into rivers."

"What? I—I don't understa—"

"What I mean is, you can come to my grandparents' house for supper." For a man who'd been manipulated by a pair of sad, blue eyes, he wasn't as angry with himself as he'd thought he would be. But he wasn't delighted, either. Glancing her way, he frowned. "Maybe we can figure out what to do."

The dog barked, almost as if to say, *I like her. If we take her in I bet she wouldn't even eat anybody's shoes.*

"Shut up, Dawg," Garth muttered, staring out the windshield. This should teach him not to roll down windows when brides came running at him.

"This is awfully nice of you." Garth heard a rustling

sound and realized she was rising to her knees. "I knew I was right about your profile."

He sensed she was about to hug him, which didn't seem like the worst idea in the world. She had a nice little figure—what he could see of it—and her mouth had a cute pout that would have been seductive under other circumstances—say, if they'd bumped into each other two-stepping at the Broken Spur.

He turned off the highway onto the country road that led to his grandparents' spread. "You're a nice person," she whispered, her voice trembling with emotion. He felt her body press against his. As her arms wrapped around his shoulders, he braced to keep from careening into a ditch. Her kiss on his jaw was warm, if a touch sisterly. "Thank you…uh, I don't even know your name."

"Gentry, sugar." He inhaled her fragrance. Light and clean. He had a feeling she wasn't wearing perfume and the smell was sweet skin and soap. "Garth Gentry."

She eased back and he was keenly aware the instant her breasts left the vicinity. Now he was sure he'd been right not to offer to take her in personally. He stirred to get more comfortable. Hell, knowing about that garter belt was having its effect. If she'd get rid of those Ph.D.-in-library-science glasses, lose a ton of prissy fabric and—

"My name's Deedee Emerson."

He nodded, deciding a subject change was in order. "Pleasure, Deedee." After a second he frowned in thought. "Deedee? You mean your married name would have been Deedee DeWinter?" He chuckled. "Sugar, that's not a name, it's a stutter."

She laughed this time, though the effort was tinged with melancholy. He shifted to look at her. She petted Old Dawg, who'd plopped his scraggly head into her lap like it was old home week and her lap was his old home.

She seemed relieved, almost relaxed. Clearly she trusted him—believed he wouldn't let her down. If she only knew. In the category "Not Letting Women Down," his record stunk.

Grandpa Perry and Grandma Clara were a different story. They were solid as oak, their hearts as big as heaven. They'd taken him in as a child, and he hadn't been any prize. And even though they were getting old and living on a shoestring, the minute they heard her story they'd make her feel as welcome as sunshine after a long, dreary winter.

This rescuing-damsels-in-distress business had its downside. Garth ground his teeth, guilt riding him hard. At the end of the weekend, he'd head back to his place on Keystone Lake, leaving the runaway bride and her troubles in his rearview mirror. But his grandparents wouldn't think of doing that. They'd keep her on for as long as she needed help.

"Damnation," he muttered.

"What?" He heard her shift toward him. "What's wrong?"

He didn't make eye contact. "Nothing."

His poor, unsuspecting grandparents. They had the mistaken notion he was only bringing them a store-bought cake.

DEEDEE COULDN'T BELIEVE that in the forty minutes since she'd bolted from the church she'd been rescued by a cowboy—of all things to find in downtown Tulsa—and had already been given refuge. Well, maybe not *given* in so many words—yet! But if Deedee Emerson was anything, she was optimistic. She looked for the best in people and situations, and when she'd seen Garth Gentry sitting at that stoplight, she'd sensed he would help her. And he had.

She faced him as he turned off the country road onto a gravel drive. "Are we there?"

He flicked her a brief look. "Almost."

She watched him maneuver around the potholes. He had a strong, rough-cut profile, like the hunky cowboys on those Marlboro billboards. His hair was thick, black and wavy, just brushing the collar of his western shirt. Dark, arched brows hovered in a slight frown over deep-set eyes.

And those lashes. They were obscenely long. She wondered if he'd be forced to clip them if he ever needed to wear glasses. If he didn't they'd drive him crazy sliding back and forth across the glass. He wouldn't be able to see half the time. She almost smiled at the outlandish image. Maybe she was lucky her lashes were stubby to the point of being a cruel trick of nature.

"There's the house," he said, drawing her out of her musings. She looked. Over the rise she could see a two-story frame home, like fifty thousand others in the Midwest countryside. It looked as if it could use a coat of paint. She shuddered inwardly as memories of her dirt-poor childhood came rushing back. Once she'd left the ranch, she'd promised herself she would never set foot outside a city again. But here she was, without options—a hop, skip and a jump away from horse manure.

They pulled to a dusty stop at the end of the gravel drive. Garth shifted around in his seat and grabbed a Stetson out of the back. Opening his door, he unfolded long, muscular legs. Deedee noticed that his jeans were starched and creased and he smelled good—like a cedar chest full of cherry tobacco.

Hopping out of the cab, he planted the hat low on his brow. Surprising her, he reached back inside. Hoisting a white bakery box from the back, he aimed earthy brown eyes her way. "You might as well get on out, sugar. This is the butler's day off."

His smart-aleck remark coupled with the fact that she'd found his eyes so fascinating made her a little cranky. Clearly he wasn't delighted by her presence and didn't intend to go out of his way to make her feel at home. She yanked on the door handle, concluding that she couldn't blame him. After all, he didn't have a sign on his pickup that read, "Runaway Brides—Feel Free to Nose-dive through my Window."

When she sprang onto the gravel, she yelped in pain, discovering she wore only one shoe. The dog clambered out and straggled off as she yanked on the trailing bridal gown so that it would clear the cab. Ducking back inside, she searched frantically. After coming up with nothing but a torn gasoline receipt and a couple of gum wrappers and a mangled bouquet of roses, she slammed the door. Bunching her frothy skirts in her arms, she checked the ground around her. Nothing. "Oh, *darn!*"

She heard crunching and looked up in time to see Garth come around the front of the truck, the white box in one hand, a saddle under the other arm. "What's wrong now?" His tone held weary misgiving.

She extended her naked foot. "I've lost a shoe."

His lips curved sardonically. "Maybe that's why Miss Manners says diving through windows isn't the best way to enter a vehicle."

Deedee dropped her skirts, miffed. "Well, the window is all you opened!"

His quick grin revealed a flash of teeth, and she found the sight irksomely attractive. "My mistake. I thought you wanted to talk, not swan dive into my lap."

She opened her mouth to retort, but heard the squeak of a door. When she spun to look, a thin woman stood on the porch. She wore jeans, boots, a short-sleeved cotton shirt, and looked to be in her seventies. Her snowy hair was straight, cropped close to her head as though the lip of a mixing bowl had determined the style. But somehow the look worked on the petite woman with bright brown eyes.

She was smiling broadly, but when her glance fell on Deedee, her expression faltered. "Land sakes, Garth!" Her gnarled hands flew to her chest. "You're married?" Turning, she shouted into the house, "Come on out here, Pa. Garth has brought home a woman!"

"You know me better than that, Grandma." Garth eyed Deedee, frustration flashing in his glance.

The door squeaked again. A tall man lumbered out. He was stoop shouldered, with a shock of wavy gray hair. His right arm was in a splint.

"What's the commotion?" the man asked in an overly loud voice, as though he didn't hear well. When he spotted Deedee, his ruddy brow wrinkled in confusion. "What's this?" he bellowed.

She colored fiercely. Now all three of them were staring at her. She knew she must be a sight in her torn and rumpled wedding dress, much of it wadded up in her arms. One shoe off and one on, she looked like Cinderella after the magic was gone. With great effort, she managed a smile.

Garth bounded up the steps. "Happy Birthday, Grandpa." He flung the saddle over the porch rail, then turned back. His grin disappeared as his gaze fell on his grandfather's injury. "Grandpa?" He fingered the sling that held the old man's arm. "What in thunder happened to you?"

Deedee watched the old rancher look down at his splint and was relieved that the focus had been shifted away from her. "Horse jammed me up against a barn wall a week or so ago,'' Perry yelled, looking sheepish. "It's comin' right along, though.''

Garth's smile had disappeared and a worried frown rode his brow. "Glad to hear it.'' Grinning again he added loudly, "I brought you something you've been wanting, Grandpa.''

Pushing his half spectacles up on his forehead, the old man squinted at Garth, then shifted his gaze to Deedee. "Lookie there, Clara,'' he shouted, nudging his wife, "the boy brought me a woman for my birthday.''

# 2

"GARTH DIDN'T BRING YOU a woman for your birthday, old man. He brought you that saddle!" The elderly woman poked her husband in the ribs. "Besides, I'm all the woman you can handle, you horny toad."

Garth's laughter was rich. "I don't want to hear this."

Deedee's smile became genuine. She liked these people. She glanced at Garth. It was evident that he loved the old couple, for their good-natured bantering had cleared the frown from his brow. He was actually smiling.

At that instant, it came to her why he'd been a little gruff on the way here. His grandparents were openhearted people. Naturally he didn't relish bringing her troubles to those he loved most in the world, knowing they would take her worries on as their own. They were obviously folks who knew no strangers, welcomed everybody like family. And they probably had troubles enough. If anybody knew how hard it was to make ends meet on a small ranch, she did.

Garth's grandmother reached toward him. "Give me that cake and introduce your pretty guest, son."

He glanced toward Deedee, his smile dimming slightly. "This is Deedee Emerson. Deedee, these are my grandparents, Clara and Perry Gentry."

She nodded. "Nice to meet you, Mr. and Mrs. Gentry."

"Likewise, dear, but call me Clara and this is—"

"*Stinkweed?*" Perry shouted. "Who'd name a pretty thing like that Stinkweed?"

"*Deedee!* Deedee Emerson!" Clara bellowed, then smiled at her. "Don't mind Pa. He can't hear squat, 'cept when you *don't* want him to hear something. Then he has ears like a cat!" She shook her head, letting out a husky laugh. "Between my arthritis and Pa being stove up and deaf as a stump, we make quite a pair." She looked at Garth. "You and this pretty thing known each other long?" Deedee could tell from the way Clara said it that she was making a sly reference to the bridal gown.

Garth crossed his arms before him and gave his grandmother a narrow look. "Do you want to hear this or would you rather make up your own story?"

She snorted. "Oh, go on. Go on."

"Thank you." He indicated Deedee with a nod. "Miss Emerson decided she didn't want to marry Tyler DeWinter, so she ran out of the church and dived through my truck window. That's about it."

"Land sakes," Clara gasped.

"What'd he say?" Perry shouted.

Clara touched her husband's arm. "Deedee dived through Garth's truck window!" she shouted.

"What'd she do that for?" Perry asked.

"Because that was all I opened," Garth said, with a teasing glance at Deedee.

Perry appeared confused and scratched his chin.

Clara's expression was pitying. "You poor little thing."

Deedee flushed. "Well…it's really okay. I realized I was making a mistake, so I left. Garth happened to be there at the right time."

"The DeWinters, of all people!" Clara sounded in awe. "They have a mighty long reach. No wonder you decided to get out of town for a spell."

Deedee shrugged. "It wasn't exactly a decision…" Not knowing what to say, she paused.

Clara shifted the cake box under an arm and waved a welcome to Deedee. "Well, enough chitchattin' out here in the heat. Come on up here, girl. Dinner's ready and you look like you could use a hot meal."

Deedee pushed her glasses more firmly up her nose, feeling shy. "I hate to impose. I know it's Perry's birthday party."

"Nonsense," Clara said. "The more the merrier. Right, Pa?"

"Who's going to marry her?" He looked at his grandson, perplexed. "Garth? This is sudden, ain't it, boy?"

Garth shook his head at his grandfather. "Let's get inside where it's cool. I'll explain during dinner." Slinging an arm around the older man, he glanced toward Deedee, who hadn't moved. With a wry crook of his lips, he lifted his other hand in invitation. "Come on, sugar."

A hot flush crept up her cheeks and she couldn't fathom why. She supposed this self-satisfied cowboy and his liberal use of intimacies had something to do with it. Oh, she realized the word *sugar* meant no more to him than "hey you," but even so, it was disconcerting for this perfect stranger to call her "sugar" every five minutes. In all her life she'd never been called anything but Deedee. Even Tyler had never used endearments like darling or sweetheart.

Hiking her dress out of her way, she hobbled to the steps, flinching every time her bare foot landed on sharp gravel. When she reached the porch, she was startled to find Garth lingering to hold the door.

Taller than she'd first imagined, he seemed to fill the entry, all shoulders and long legs. Suddenly restless, she cleared her throat. Not only did he have an honest profile, he had a sexy body. The idea of slipping past him seemed almost illicit. *Fool!* her brain reprimanded, *he's just holding the door!* Shaking off the ridiculous idea, she clomped un-evenly by, quipping, "I thought it was the butler's day off."

Garth shut the door and stepped into the room, his glance snagging hers. "I like to think Grandma raised a gentle-man."

"Really? Where does she keep him?" She didn't mean that. He'd behaved like a gentleman so far—on the whole. There was just something about this cowboy that brought out a sauciness in her that she had hardly been aware ex-isted.

Garth's chuckle was deep and pleasant as he hung his hat on a coatrack beside the staircase. "Is that any way to talk to the man who rescued you from the trauma of mar-rying into one of the wealthiest families in Oklahoma?"

She experienced a stab at the reminder, and it must have shown on her face, for his grin faded. "Sorry." Surprising her, he took her elbow, steering her into the parlor.

The pale, rosebud-patterned wallpaper looked to be of a fifties vintage, as was the furniture. Plain and sparse, the room reminded Deedee of her childhood, and her hand-to-mouth existence on her father's ranch. She'd hated the chores that had kept her from having fun and joining in after-school activities. Her clothes had always been charity giveaways and she'd been laughed at by her peers. At nine-teen, when her father died, she'd sold the place for prac-tically nothing and vowed never to set foot on a ranch again.

A shudder of distaste ran through her at the memory, and she hated herself for feeling anything so uncharitable in a home that was clearly a haven of kindness and goodwill.

"Not much like the DeWinters' place?" Garth asked, sounding as though he'd read her thoughts in her expression and stiffened posture.

She shook her head, noticing several photos of him on the mantel—all on horseback. He looked every inch a cowboy, from the top of his Stetson to the toes of his Roper boots.

"You two coming?" Clara called, and Deedee looked up. The dining room was at the rear of the parlor. Beyond the archway, the older woman stood beside an oak table crowded with food. The smell of fried chicken wafted through the air.

"Be right there." Garth aimed Deedee toward the dining room. "Let's eat, Miss Emerson."

She tugged on his hold. "In this?" She indicated her torn and rumpled gown.

He scanned her with a critical squint. "Why? Do you usually eat in the nude?"

She gaped at him for a moment before she found her voice. "That's *not* what I meant."

"I know what you meant, sugar," he assured her. "But if you recall, you don't have anything else to put on." He took her elbow again.

She hobbled two more steps and then sighed. "Would you mind if I take off my shoe? I'm getting dizzy."

"Suit yourself."

She started to kick it off, but had second thoughts. "You won't make comments about how taking off my shoe is a sign I want to eat in the nude, will you?"

"Me?" His expression was almost believable in its surprise. "No, ma'am. I'm a regular Boy Scout."

His soft tone, the gleam in his eyes, caused something in the pit of her stomach to tighten. *Boy Scout, my patoot!* Her woman's intuition told her that he'd be a whole lot of trouble for any female who let her heart get tangled up with his. Luckily she didn't have plans in that direction. Ranchers were a rung below ax murderers on her men-I-want-to-become-involved-with list. "I think you've confused the Boy Scouts with the Navy," she said, drawing her elbow from his grasp. "It's sailors who have a girl in every port, not Boy Scouts."

His flash of teeth did something odd to her breathing. "You wound me, sugar. Someday, if you're real nice, I'll show you my good-conduct badge."

She eyed heaven. Good conduct or not, she couldn't deny that his charm had an effect. Somehow running out on Ty seemed less disgraceful now, and her nagging guilt diminished a shade. She silently thanked Garth's easygoing manner for that. When he made the effort, he could put a woman at ease. "You're in a better mood," she said.

He glanced at her. "I was just thinking the same about you."

She indicated his grandparents, as they seated themselves. "They're darling. I guess they rubbed off on me."

He looked at the couple and nodded. She could see his love for them in his eyes, a pleasant sight. "They are great, aren't they?"

"You didn't want to involve them in my problems."

He peered at her, a brow lifting at her discerning remark. "Do you blame me?"

She inhaled, glad to get it out in the open. "Not at all. I'd feel the same way."

"They're going to take you in, you know," he said.

"I know." She smiled in gratitude. "And I promise, I'll be a big help while I'm here."

One dark eyebrow lifted skeptically. "I believe you."

She laughed out loud, amazed that she could after the day she'd had. "You liar! You still think I'm crazy."

"No, I don't," he drawled, then paused. "Well..." A faint light twinkled in the depths of those earthy eyes. "Let's just say I don't figure you're dangerous."

AFTER HELPING WITH the dishes, Deedee gratefully accepted some of Clara's clothes. She felt more at home in a pair of jeans and a T-shirt that read Over What Hill? Orange balletlike bedroom slippers served as her shoes. She looked down at herself, adjusting her glasses. She might not be in the running for the cover of *Vogue,* but she was comfortable, and she blessed the elderly woman's kindness.

"Here, child," Clara said. "Let's take our coffee into the parlor. Garth should have his horse bedded down by now, so the men ought to be coming in real soon."

Deedee took her mug off the old pine counter and followed Clara into the short hallway that led to the parlor. "That was a beautiful saddle Garth gave Perry," she commented.

"He made it." Clara's voice was filled with pride. "Seems everything that boy touches turns gold." She indicated the rust-colored couch with crocheted doilies on each arm. "Did you know, he's won every top cutting competition there is—more than a few times—from the NCHA World—"

"Don't bore the lady, Grandma." Garth appeared from the kitchen hallway, his features grim.

"What's wrong, son?"

He shook his head at her. "Grandma, do I have to turn you over my knee?"

Clara had lifted her mug from the coffee table, but she plunked it down, looking perturbed. "I didn't raise you to sass your grandmother, boy."

His jaw worked. "I didn't leave you two here alone to kill yourselves doing chores you can't handle. Grandpa can't do a darned thing with that bunged-up arm. You should have told me."

"I shoulda done no such thing. Besides, he's an old pain in the neck and wouldn't let me."

Settling his rangy body in an easy chair facing the couch, Garth leaned forward, looking intent. "I should give you an extra swat for not telling me your hired man ran off last week."

Clara made a dismissive gesture with gnarled, arthritic hands. "We lose hired men all the time. Somebody else'll come along."

Garth closed his eyes. Deedee could tell by the bunching of his jaw muscles that he was fighting frustration. "What am I going to do with you two?"

"You have your own life, boy. We're fine."

Deedee took a sip of coffee as he opened his eyes and sternly scanned his grandmother. "You're fine, all right. Fine as two baby chicks looking down the throat of a fox."

"Mind your business," Clara said in the same stern tone. "You're not so big I can't tan that backside of yours."

His lips quirked, but there was less amusement in the expression than exasperation. "What do you expect to do, chase me around the barn with that rug beater?"

"I've done it before."

"I was six."

"Don't you sass me. I'll wait till you're asleep and safety-pin you to your bed and whack the stuffing out of you with my *Geographic*. I did it to your grandpa when he gambled away the egg money in '52, and I can do it again."

Garth sat up. "That's mean talk, but it's not going to do you any good. I'm staying on until Grandpa's out of that splint, and I won't hear any arguments." He stood up. "Coffee smells good. I think I'll have some."

"You'll do no such of a thing!"

"It's settled." He headed toward the kitchen.

"Pa'll have a fit!" she shouted.

"You let me worry about that."

When he was gone, Clara sat back, shaking her head. "That boy." She sighed long and low.

Setting down her cup, Deedee asked, "Can he leave his place just like that?"

Clara nodded. "He's got help."

Deedee gave Clara a penetrating look. She seemed awfully relaxed for a woman who'd just threatened her grandson with bodily harm. Then the truth dawned on Deedee. "You knew he'd stay, didn't you. You *wanted* him to."

The older woman peered sideways at her and grinned like a cat full of cream. "He's a good boy."

Deedee was amazed. "Why, you little conniver."

Clara's laugh was husky. "You know men, child. They like to think things is their idea." She glanced at Deedee and winked. "What they don't know won't hurt 'em."

Deedee took a sip of her coffee, growing fidgety. "Of course I won't stay, then. I mean, it was nice of you to offer, but you won't have room for—"

"Nonsense, child," Clara patted her arm. "There's plenty of room." She leaned close. "Besides, you're already paying for yourself."

"I am?"

"Sure. That trick you taught me about rubbing sticky zippers with a lead pencil to get them unstuck." She squeezed Deedee's knee. "I was gonna throw out those jeans, but since you got them unstuck they're fine. It's only fair I loan them to you for a spell."

Deedee flushed. "That's part of my job."

"What's part of your job?" Garth asked as he returned with two mugs of coffee, his grandfather shuffling along behind.

"Getting jeans unzipped," Clara chirped, grinning.

Garth glanced from his grandmother to Deedee, his expression quizzical. "I'm fascinated." He set one of the mugs on the coffee table before he resumed his seat in the chair. "Tell me more about zippers."

Perry flicked on the TV. "*Flipper?* I love that show," he yelled. "But I think all we got now is news."

"No, *zipper,* Pa!" Clara shouted.

"I heard ya, woman." He waved a big paw toward the TV. "If you're that set on it, I'll check the channels."

When Clara started to shout out "zipper" again, Deedee put a hand on her shoulder. "Let's forget it. TV sounds like a good idea."

She could feel Garth's gaze on her while she turned crimson, and she had a horrible feeling his eyes were twinkling with fun at her expense. When she could get up her nerve, she frowned at him, making it clear that she didn't appreciate his taunting. His answering wink was infuriating, but she decided to keep her comments to herself. He might be a gentleman in some ways, but he was also an incorrigible tease.

As the TV warmed up, Perry roared, "Clara, did the boy tell you he's planning to stay on until I get out of this splint?"

"He told me," she shouted back. "I told you he would."

The old man reached for his coffee. "He's an ornery cuss, that boy. I don't know where he gets it from."

"Ha!" Clara retorted. "I've seen you stare down a prairie fire, you old mule. Where do you think he gets it from?"

"*Me?*" Perry wagged a blunt finger at his wife. "You'd gripe if you was hung with a new rope, woman!"

Deedee smiled at their good-natured bickering—though she made a mental note not to sit between them next time. It was a good way to go deaf.

"Hey," Garth interrupted. "Look who's on TV."

Deedee's smile died when she saw her own image fill the screen. It was the wedding picture she'd turned in to the paper. The photographer had convinced her not to wear her glasses, and she'd had her hair done that morning. The picture was soft focus and flattering. Nobody would recognize her on the street from that photograph.

"In the middle of the ceremony," the reporter was saying, "Miss Emerson bolted from the church and, according to eye witnesses, jumped into a passing truck. Her whereabouts are unknown. A DeWinter family spokesman stated that Tyler DeWinter has left the state for an undetermined location, and that he had no comment."

Garth chuckled. "From where I was sitting he had a comment."

Deedee's face was so hot she was afraid she would spontaneously combust. "Would you mind if we turned that off?" she whispered.

Garth pushed up from the chair. "No problem."

"Why'd you do that, boy?" Perry shouted.

Clara reached across Deedee and swatted his leg. "Hush, Mr. Insensitive!" She shifted to Deedee, patting her knee. "That was a lovely picture of you, dear. I admire you for having the gumption to run out like that. You've got spunk." She turned to her grandson. "Don't you think she has spunk, Garth?"

"Absolutely." He leveled his gaze on Deedee as he sat back down. "Aunt Jessie had spunk, too. 'Course, we had to put her in a home."

"Garth!" Clara admonished.

He grinned, glancing at his watch. "It's getting late. Maybe we ought to turn in."

"Fine idea." Clara agreed. "You show Deedee her room."

Unsure why the idea of Garth taking her to a bedroom made her nervous, Deedee blurted, "I'd better clean up the rest of the dishes."

"Land sakes no, girl," Clara said. "It's just four mugs. I'll leave 'em in the sink for morning."

Garth got up and extended a hand. "Come on, Spunky. I'll show you the way."

"Get her some clean sheets out of the linen closet, son."

"Yes, ma'am." Garth took Deedee's arm, aiming her toward the foyer and the stairs.

She nervously fingered her glasses. This was such a touchy-feely family. Clara kept patting her and Garth kept taking her arm. Deedee wasn't sure she could get used to it—especially Garth's touch. There was something electrical about it that unsettled her. She tried to make light of the situation and ignore the feel of his hand at her elbow, saying, "You can call me Spunky all you please, but I won't go to a nuthouse."

Low laughter rumbled in his chest. "That's thinking positive."

She pulled her lips between her teeth. Making light wasn't working. Her body still registered his touch with dogged singularity. She pulled from his grasp. "Look, if—if my room's upstairs, you don't have to lead me. I'm not two years old."

"Can't help it. It's the gentleman in me." His fingers curled around her wrist as he coaxed her up the stairs. "But if it makes you uncomfortable…"

She swallowed. "Don't be silly. I'm completely comfortable."

"Whatever you say, sugar." When they reached the second floor, he indicated the first room. "That's mine. The one beside it's yours." He released her to knuckle the door at her back. "That's the bathroom, and next to it, Grandpa and Grandma's room." Taking her arm again, he led her the few paces to her door. "You go on in and I'll get the sheets."

"Don't be silly," she protested. "I'll get the sheets. Where are they?"

"You keep calling me silly, sugar, and I'll get a complex." He indicated the linen closet, at the end of the hall between her room and his grandparents'. "There are towels in there, too." He started to leave, then turned back. "Say, what about a shower, sugar?"

She stared, stunned. "Are you crazy? I hardly know you!"

His lips twitched. "Yep, I feel a complex coming on. Now I'm not just silly, but crazy, too."

She planted her fists on her hips. "I realize I owe you a lot, but I'm not in the habit of showering with men I've just met."

Running a hand over his mouth, he cleared his throat. "That's a real shame, sugar, but what I was asking was do *you* plan to take a shower tonight?" Amusement lit his eyes as he lost his fight not to grin. "There's just the one bathroom, and I usually take my shower at night."

She spun away, horrified at herself. "Oh..." Swinging open the linen closet door, she blindly fished among clean-smelling sheets. "Go—go ahead," she mumbled. "I won't be needing..." Her voice died away in mortification. *Please,* her mind screamed, *while I'm not looking, bash me with something and put me out of my misery!*

"Gentleman that I am, I'll be going now." His voice was liberally tinged with laughter.

She groaned, leaning her forehead into the sheets. Where was a freight train when you needed one? She longed to be run over and turned into railroad track ooze—it had to be less painful than this!

# 3

DEEDEE HAD MIXED EMOTIONS about staying with the Gentrys. Every sight, sound and smell reminded her of her childhood. On the positive side, however, she had a roof over her head, good food, and she was crazy about Perry and Clara.

The most daunting thing about this whole setup—worse even than being back on a hand-to-mouth ranch—was having Garth underfoot all day. He bothered her. He bothered her with that smile, those twinkling eyes and that devil-may-care attitude. Standing at the kitchen window, she looked toward the barn, watching in dreaded fascination as he chopped up a dead oak. It didn't take her long to discover one more aspect of the man that bothered her.

Every time his ax fell, she swallowed hard. His back glistened in the afternoon heat. Muscles that she'd never known existed bulged. Well, she knew there were muscles in a person's back. Anybody who'd had high school biology knew there were muscles everywhere in the human body. Besides, she'd seen backache commercials on TV that graphically showed those muscles, usually with lightning bolts shooting out of them. But she'd never seen back muscles bulge and glisten as impressively as at that moment—in Garth's back. Not to mention his shoulders and arms, powerful and glossy in the sunshine.

"He's a nice-looking boy, isn't he?"

Deedee nearly dropped the bowl she'd been holding.

Since she'd been absentmindedly rubbing it for the past five minutes, she decided it was dry. Turning, she smiled timidly at Clara, who had entered the kitchen. "I—I was finishing up the lunch dishes." Trying to appear nonchalant, she asked, "What did you say?"

Clara smiled and joined her at the window. "I said he's a nice-looking boy."

Deedee chewed the inside of her cheek. Only his grandmother could call that hunk a boy. "I—I suppose. Sure."

The older woman took the bowl from her hand. "He's a bad one, though, where women are concerned."

Deedee was startled to hear Clara say anything negative about her grandson, and peered at her. "Bad?"

Clara put the bowl under a counter. "What I mean is, he's a heartbreaker, that boy." She turned back, shaking her head. "Don't take me wrong. I love him. But he's got it in his head he's not cut out for harness. He was married once. Ten years ago, when he was twenty-five."

"Really?" Deedee looked out the window with forced casualness.

"Pretty little thing, too. But Garth had his head into his cutting horses, travelin' all over to competitions. When he was home, he spent his time training his cutters. Like lots of women would, she felt neglected. Ran off on Garth's twenty-seventh birthday. Found herself a nice, safe bookkeeper."

Clara walked to a hook on the wall beside the window and took down an apron. "The sorry thing about it was, her leaving didn't bother Garth much. It's strange, but he took it harder not minding her leaving than the leavin' itself." She tied the red-checked apron around her waist. "He never said it in so many words, but I figure he decided he wasn't cut out for marriage, since he didn't hurt like he should have. So he plays the field."

Deedee watched him as he split another piece of wood. "Well—if he's happy, that's what counts, right?" She smiled at Clara, not wanting the woman to think that the attraction of a few muscles meant she had any long-term plans for Garth. She certainly didn't. "If you can be happy, that's what's important."

Clara nodded, looking thoughtful. "I suppose. But it doesn't seem natural, him flitting from flower to flower all his life. I'm afraid he'll end up a lonely old man. I don't like to think about that."

Deedee's heart went out to the woman and she put an arm around her thin shoulders. "That's the hardest part about loving somebody—you can't force them to do what they don't want to do, even if you know it's better for them." She recalled all the times she'd begged her father to give up the ranch, take a job in town. But he'd had it in his head that he wasn't cut out for city life, and fought till his dying day to make his ranch a success, never quite managing.

Clara looked at Deedee, her expression soft. "You're a wise little thing for your years, girl. I like you." She slid her arm about Deedee's waist. "You know what? I'm feeling so perky after those forty winks you made me take, I have a hankering to make some apple pies. If you'll peel the apples, child. I can't handle that chore with these old hands."

"I'm a great peeler." Deedee's spirits lifted with Clara's gratitude.

"First, girl…" She opened the refrigerator and took out a frosty jug of water. "I'd be grateful if you'd take this out to Garth. I asked Pa to do it on his way to the barn, but as usual, he didn't hear me."

Deedee experienced a tingle of excitement and squelched it. She did *not* intend to be titillated by the idea of being near a cowboy—especially one who intended to spend his life flitting from flower to flower.

Unfortunately for the unsuspecting females of the world, Garth Gentry had the looks and charisma to do all the pollinating he had the strength for. Any woman would give her eyeteeth to run her hands over those sexy muscles.

With a frail smile, she nodded at Clara. "Sure...sure. I'll take it right away." She scurried out the kitchen door, hoping the blush creeping up her cheeks hadn't given away her wanton thoughts. "Boy, Tyler, did you get lucky when I ran out of that church!" she muttered. "If I can have risqué thoughts about a *cowboy,* there was no hope for our marriage!"

She passed the vegetable garden, with its neatly weeded rows of tomatoes, green beans, beets and cabbages. The backyard sloped toward the old oak barn, its red paint fading. A chicken coop stood to the right of the barn, the chickens scratching around behind their fence, clucking and squawking. On the other side of the barn several mama cows and their calves lingered in the shade of the loafing shed. Others meandered in the pasture, their babies tagging close behind.

Oak, hickory and hackberry trees dotted the flat landscape, waving in a hot June breeze. Birds twittered in the branches, and the shrill whir of the katydid's song seemed to come from everywhere. Things didn't change much, she decided with a shiver of remembrance.

The grass under her ballet slippers was stiff and dry, unlike the patches of green around her apartment house, where sprinklers watered the lawn every other night so the earth wouldn't become parched the way it would naturally during most Oklahoma summers.

The tree stump where Garth worked was about halfway between the house and the barn. Finally, reluctantly, her gaze fell on his broad, sun-bronzed back. That hadn't changed much, either, since she'd stared at him through the kitchen window. He swung his ax in a long arc, his muscles bunching and flexing, shiny and sexy. With a solid whack the ax blade sliced through another section of limb as though through warm butter.

As the pieces clattered off the cutting stump, she called out, "Time for a water break, Garth."

Shoulders hunched in the act of reaching for another chunk of wood, he peered in her direction. He'd tied a red bandanna around his brow to keep stinging sweat out of his eyes. He turned to greet her. His hair was damp and mussed, his grin debilitating.

She sucked in an appreciative breath and stumbled. Her misstep was so brief she didn't think he'd seen it. Nevertheless, she attempted to mask her blunder with a hearty wave. "You're pretty good at that," she called. "I bet you've done it before."

He leaned the ax against the stump. "More times than I care to count." His chest expanded as he inhaled. Curling chest hair glistened, trailing seductively down his belly to disappear below the waistband of his jeans. Giving her eyes a direct order, she yanked her attention to his face and kept it there. His taut, male stomach was none of her concern.

When she reached him, he took the jug from her outstretched hand. "Thanks." As he tipped the bottle to his lips, Deedee was disconcerted to notice his gaze lingering on her. She began to doubt the wisdom of tying the knot in Clara's T-shirt, exposing her midriff. She had to battle an urge to untie it. After several long swallows, he lowered the jug. "You look cool," he remarked, pouring water into his hand, then splashing his face with it.

She didn't know how to respond. First of all, it was more of a comment than a compliment. And secondly, her scru-

tiny—and her thoughts—had followed the water as it drib-
bled onto his chest, swirling and darting, forming twinkling
little paths through his chest hair.

She swallowed, forcing herself to recall his remark. *Answer him, you ninny!* her brain screamed. She squinted,
perturbed with herself. What had he said—something about
her looking cool? Oh, right! "I, uh, I hear that's what air
conditioners are for."

"Ah." He nodded, gulping down the rest of the water.
"What have you and Grandma been up to?" He handed
her the empty jug.

"We're going to make apple pies."

His brows quirked. "No kidding?" He eyed her speculatively, planting one fist on a hip. "Can you cook?"

She dragged her gaze from the play of muscles the move
incited. "Uh, I can peel."

He grinned. "I bet you can, sugar." Turning away, he
picked up the ax and grabbed another chunk of wood, setting it on its end. With a glance her way, he winked.
"Thanks, again—for the water."

She was startled to realize she'd been rooted there like
a dandelion, staring at his back. Only when he'd winked
had she sensed how stupid she must have looked. Darn
those muscles and their weird hypnotic effect.

Swallowing, she took a step backward. "Uh, sure—no
problem."

He lifted his ax. As it swung down to cleave the piece
of oak, Deedee spun toward the house. Why did everything
the man said or did seem like a come-on? Was he coming
on to her? Did she want him to?

Chewing her lower lip, she tromped toward the house.
Fidgeting fingers went to the knot at her side. Undoing it,
she answered her own question. No, she didn't want this
cowboy coming on to her. The exposed midriff might have

given him the wrong signals. She vowed from now on to broadcast nothing but loose, baggy, Hands Off, You Serial Flower Pollinator, You! messages.

She'd almost made a bad mistake by letting Tyler's money blind her to what she really wanted out of marriage. She didn't intend to let some fly-by-night cowboy's sex appeal blur her thinking, either.

Her father may not have given her much, but over the years he'd shared recollections with her of his happiest times with her mother. When he'd spoken of Marianne, his eyes had glimmered with devotion. Her father had never remarried after Marianne's death, preferring to live with his memories.

That was the kind of love Deedee wanted—the eternal kind, sustaining you through life's toughest times. She hadn't felt that way about Tyler, and it was clear that Garth didn't intend to be anybody's eternal love, so she didn't plan to get all fluttery about him.

She swung open the kitchen door, banishing visions of Garth's sexy back and taunting grin from her thoughts. She had her whole life ahead of her. Today she would peel apples with Clara and learn how to make an apple pie. And someday, down the road, she'd run smack into a wonderful man—a solid noncowboy she could love with all her heart and soul. A man who would give her love for all eternity. She wasn't worried.

AFTER DINNER Perry and Clara settled at the dining room table for a quiet game of checkers. At least they'd said it would be quiet.

"Who taught you to play checkers, old woman?"

"Who do you think? Or are you losing your *mind*, too?"

"What difference does it make, what *time* it is? You

catching a bus? Now don't make that move, I'm telling you—"

"There! I've done it. King me!"

"Cheat!" Perry yelled. "I won't king you!"

Garth's low laugh wafted across the room to Deedee, and she looked up from applying alcohol to the Gentrys' old phone.

He sat cross-legged on the rag rug, playing pull the sock with his dog. "The folks are cute, aren't they?"

Deedee smiled. "They enjoy checkers, do they?"

Dawg growled and yanked on the sock. "I'm afraid this is their idea of foreplay," Garth said. His grin was wry.

Startled by the comment, Deedee couldn't hold back a giggle. She dabbed more alcohol on the phone and rubbed it around.

Garth eyed her dubiously. "I didn't know the telephone had been wounded."

She gave the receiver one last swipe and settled the phone on the end table where it belonged. "For your information, cleaning your telephone with rubbing alcohol keeps it looking new."

He glanced at the black, plastic relic. "You're asking a lot from a phone with an I Like Ike sticker on it." Garth let his mutt take the sock, which Dawg promptly shook as if it were a vanquished foe.

"What was *that*, old man?" Clara screeched.

"If you can move sideways, I can move sideways!"

Deedee folded her rag and picked up the alcohol bottle. "Maybe we should leave them alone."

Garth placed his hands on his knees. "I thought you'd never ask, sugar. There's a place not far from here called the Broken Spur. Do you two-step?"

She felt that ugly little quiver of excitement again and clenched her teeth. "Uh...well, that's not exactly what I had in mind.'' She indicated the direction of the kitchen. ''I'll be right back. I need to put these away.''

When she returned, Garth was squinting at her, his brows dipping speculatively. ''What did you have in mind?''

His voice was low and seductive, and that annoyed her. Well, not his voice, exactly, just her Wahoo-let's-go-baby! reaction to the simple question. *No,* she told herself. *Not him. You'd be nothing to this cowboy, Deedee Emerson, but one more sexual conquest in a huge bouquet of sexual conquests. Tie up your libido, kick it into the cellar of your brain and forget about it!*

''Lie down!''

Garth's command jarred her out of her reverie, and she blinked at him, stunned that he would issue such a lusty order in front of his grandparents. She opened her mouth to retort, but realized he wasn't looking at her. He rubbed Dawg's head. Wadding the sock, he tossed it to the floor. ''No more playing, fella. Now, lie down.'' Circling once, then twice near Garth's leg, the mutt settled on the rug.

Deedee started when Garth's brown eyes met hers. She felt guilty that he'd caught her staring, and thunderstruck that she'd thought...well, *what* she'd thought. ''What is it you have in mind?'' he repeated, looking sexy and cuddly in freshly washed jeans and a black knit shirt that hugged his torso like a jealous bride. His eyes were at half-mast, those long lashes hiding any thought going through his head.

''I—I was hoping you'd take me to Tulsa so I could get my clothes.''

He leaned against the easy chair, resting an elbow on the seat. ''Now?''

She shrugged, tugging on the T-shirt. ''I can't go on wearing this forever. I left some stuff in my old apartment with my ex-roommate. I expected to collect it after the honeymoon, but now..."

He pursed his lips. "Right. Okay, sugar. It's not quite what I had in mind for a Saturday night, but let's go."

She experienced a thrill of relief. "Oh—thanks."

He winked, his half grin easy. "Hey, Grandma and Grandpa," he shouted, walking into the dining room.

When they faced him with questioning expressions, he said, "I'm taking Deedee into Tulsa to get some clothes from her old apartment." He bent down to kiss his grandmother's cheek. "If you want to chase each other around naked, you've got a couple of hours."

Clara's husky laugh rang out and she playfully slapped Garth's arm. "You're bad."

"There's a snake in the shower?" Perry shouted.

"Game's over, Pa," Clara yelled, grabbing his hand. "Let's go look for that snake."

Garth laughed, beckoning to Deedee. "We'd better get out of here before it gets strange."

Blushing, she caught up with him. When he took her arm she didn't pull away and wondered at herself. *Don't get weak, Deedee!* she admonished inwardly. *Remember, he's a career pollinator.*

Forty-five minutes later, Garth parked his pickup in southeast Tulsa in front of a tidy, two-story complex of colonial-style apartments. All was quiet, with security lights shining at intervals along the sidewalks. Deedee didn't know what she'd expected—armed guards checking ID's to make sure no one by the name of Deedee Emerson set foot on DeWinter property?

"It's the upstairs unit on the east end," she whispered, pointing.

"Check," Garth whispered. "Why are we whispering?"

She chewed on her lower lip. "I don't know." Getting

up on her knees, she turned to look behind the seat. Spying Garth's Stetson and a pair of sunglasses, she grabbed them and shoved the latter on over her glasses. "Do you have that bandanna in your pocket?" When she put on his hat it slipped so far down it covered her ears.

He eyed her with amusement, then shifted to retrieve the bandanna from his hip pocket. "Here."

She shook it out, folded it into a triangle, then tied it at her neck, pulling the cloth up over her mouth and nose. "Okay, let's go," she whispered.

Garth's lips twitched. "Since you're dressed for it, why don't we rob a bank on the way home?"

"Shush!" She shoved his big sunglasses back into place. "Are you going to help me or make jokes?"

"I'll help. Just one thing..." He slid the sunglasses off her nose, tossing them behind the seat. "It might be a good idea if you could see." Opening his door, he stepped out, then turned back. "Coming?"

Caught off guard by his sudden exit from the truck, she nodded vigorously, the Stetson bobbing into her eyes. Righting the hat, she opened her door and slid out.

When he joined her on the sidewalk, he asked, "Do you have a key?"

She shook her head, feeling the hat wobble and slide. "No. But Alberta and I keep a spare under the mat."

He tugged the bandanna down to her chin and she left it there, deciding she was in more danger of being shot as a robber than being recognized as Tyler DeWinter's runaway bride. "Why not just hang a sign on the door that says Free Stuff?" he muttered, taking her arm and steering her toward the apartment.

"Well, we used to hide a key in a planter, but somebody stole that. Luckily, the key wasn't in it at the time."

He glanced at her, his grin a white flash in the darkness. "Ain't city life grand?"

She eyed him with disdain, but didn't say anything for they had reached the outside staircase to the second level. Her heart pounded deafeningly against her ribs.

"What about this roommate?" Garth asked.

Deedee spun around, shushing him. "She works nights." She sprinted up the steps, beating him to the door. As she bent to retrieve the key, the Stetson tumbled off. "Oh, darn."

She grabbed for it, but Garth caught it first. "Give me that damn thing." He planted it on his head, taking the key from her fingers. Before she knew it the door was unlocked and he was pushing her inside. "You make a lousy burglar, sugar."

"It's not exactly a career goal," she muttered.

He closed the door and she flipped on the light. The place was typical of a million apartments, with ecru walls and carpet, furniture in blah grays and browns, giving the dwelling all the warmth of a motel room.

One thing was different since Deedee was there last. The place was a wreck. Clothes were strewn everywhere. Magazines and panty hose shared space on the couch with an open pizza box containing two dried, curling pieces of pepperoni.

"I was wrong," Garth said with a derisive laugh. "This place is in no danger of being robbed. No thief could find anything in here."

Deedee exhaled tiredly, gazing at the wreckage. "Alberta isn't very neat."

He ambled to the coffee table and with a crooked finger scooped up a black lace bra. "What does she do when she's working nights?"

"She's a nurse's aide at St. Francis. Not every person with a double-D cup is a stripper."

He dropped the bra. "Did I say anything?"

"Not yet," she said tightly. "Why don't you stay out here and chat with...*them*...while I get packed." She picked her way through the debris and headed into the bedroom that had been hers. Once inside, she heard a familiar sound—a chittering—and her heart leaped. "Magnolia!"

She ran to the cage, half-covered by one of Alberta's cast-off slips. Tossing the garment aside, she opened the cage door and took her ferret into her arms for a hug and a kiss. "Oh, honey, I missed you, too. Kissy, kissy, Mama."

Magnolia nuzzled her neck, chittering with delight.

"You missed me too, didn't you, sweetie?" Scanning the cage, her glance took in a troubling fact: There was hardly any water. "Oh, baby. Was mean old Alberta neglecting you?"

"Who in the hell are you talking to?" Garth appeared at the door.

Deedee stood up, animosity swelling inside her. "It's Magnolia. Alberta said she'd keep her for me, but she's not taking care of her. There's barely any water in her cage."

Garth eyed the slender silver creature with a jaundiced eye. "You don't mean you're planning to take that thing?"

Deedee gave Magnolia a kiss on her little pink nose and returned her to her home. Plucking the water bottle from its perch, she hurried to the bathroom to fill it. "Of course I'm taking Magnolia. If I leave her here, Alberta might let her starve or dehydrate."

She came out of the bathroom, facing Garth. His scowl was a fair indication that he wasn't one hundred percent in favor of this idea. "She won't be any trouble. She stays in her cage most of the time." Returning the bottle to its place, she cooed, "Okay, Maggie, honey, there's your water. Mama's going to get you out of this hellhole."

"Please tell me you're releasing that thing into the wild."

"Of course not. That would be cruel." Deedee grew nervous. "You—you will let me bring her with me, won't you?"

He lifted his hat and ran a hand through his hair, replacing the Stetson low on his brow. "I don't know how Grandma and Grandpa will take this four-legged addition."

She lifted the cage, carrying it over so that he could get a better look at Magnolia. "They won't be able to resist. See those big, burgundy eyes? Isn't she sweet?"

"Sugar, there are things in the country that would love to eat that critter, burgundy eyes and all."

Repelled by the thought, Deedee gasped. "She won't leave my room."

His long exhalation spoke loudly of his frustration, but Deedee sensed he was weakening. "Please," she said, holding up the cage so he could get an eyeball view.

"Okay, okay," Garth muttered, taking the cage from her and setting it down. "Just don't let that rat kill my dog."

"Magnolia wouldn't hurt a fly." Deedee planted her hands on her hips. "And she's *not* a rat. Ferrets were brought to this country for rodent control, so don't call my darling baby a rat!"

Garth crossed his arms before him and lounged against the doorjamb, his expression disgruntled. "On one condition."

"What?"

"That you're packed in ten minutes."

Magnolia stood up on her hind legs and chattered at him, and Deedee experienced a surge of relief. "She's saying she forgives you." Deedee spun to start packing. "And I'll be done in *nine*." The sooner she was out of Alberta's pigsty the better. "Oh, Garth," she called as she pulled things from drawers, "would you leave Alberta a note? Tell her I've taken Magnolia and I'll be back for the rest of my things as soon as I find a place to live and a job."

"Where do you suggest I find a piece of paper?" he asked from the doorway.

"Use your imagination."

Eight and one-half minutes later, she came out of her bedroom carrying a suitcase in one hand and Magnolia's cage in the other. Garth was finishing the note.

"That took you long enough," she said. "Or were you writing love poetry to her brassiere?"

He shifted his head, his eyes shadowed by his hat brim. Laying aside the paper and pen, he said, "Actually, I didn't think to look in the freezer for paper right away. That's where I found a notebook." He curled his little finger around a pair of lacy red panties and held them up for her to see. "I found these in there, too."

Her cheeks blazed. "Uh, Alberta gets hot. She thinks if she freezes—"

"Don't tell me," Garth interrupted, laughter in his voice. "I want to remember Alberta just the way I found her."

Deedee shook her head at him. "If you can tear yourself away from Al's underthings, there's a bag of Magnolia's food and some litter in the entry closet."

He unfolded himself from the couch. "Do you think hot little Alberta-of-the-double-D will find the note?"

Deedee shrugged. "Eventually—when she needs underwear."

Moments later, they were in the truck heading back to the ranch, Magnolia's cage on Deedee's lap. "I really appreciate this." She looked down at her pet, curled in her hammock, looking contented. A few more days with Alberta and who knows what sort of shape Magnolia might have been in. Gritting her teeth, Deedee muttered, "That Alberta is a piece of work!"

"I liked her, too," Garth said.

She glared at his profile. He was smiling that crooked, teasing smile. For some demented reason she couldn't help but smile, too. "You're very funny."

"Hey, sugar, she was *your* roommate."

"It was pure economics. I found an apartment I liked, but I couldn't afford the rent. So I advertised."

"And you got hot Alberta." He chuckled.

"What's funny?"

"I was wondering what you did the first time you found her panties in the freezer."

She winced at the memory, pushing her glasses into place. "Well, I didn't carry them around with me drooling, like you did."

"I wasn't drooling."

She shifted to eye him dubiously. "Oh, really? Then what were you doing?"

He glanced her way and the smoldering gleam in his eyes startled her. Or was it merely the reflection of a streetlight? "If you want the truth, sugar…" His lips twitched, but he didn't quite smile. "I was hoping they were yours."

# 4

GARTH WATCHED Deedee's eyes. Her glasses flashed, reflecting a street lamp. Once they'd passed the light, her eyes were visible, and they were gigantic. The way she reacted to a little sexual innuendo amused him. If she'd laughed and teased back, it wouldn't have been as much fun. But Deedee Emerson was a spunky, tightly wound little challenge, and eliciting that wide blue stare was like winning a prize. He probably shouldn't tease her, but she teased so easily.

"You wanted the truth, sugar," he drawled.

She harrumped. "There's this tiny little area between the truth and lying," she muttered. "It's called keeping your mouth shut."

He choked back a laugh, forcing his gaze to the road. "What fun is that?"

"You place too big an emphasis on having fun, cowboy."

He shrugged. She wasn't far off. He'd never worked at anything he didn't enjoy. He'd loved training cutting horses and had made good money as a contestant. After he'd won every national honor he could win, he'd grown bored. Now he was doing fine putting his champion cutting horse out to stud and selling its foals now and then. And though saddle making had begun as an entertaining hobby, it was becoming a lucrative business. Garth loved what he did, and as long as it interested him, he'd keep doing it. "If you can't have fun, sugar, what's the point?"

Her exhalation held the fervor of a curse. "If you don't know, then I'm certainly not going to explain."

"It'd be a waste of energy." He winked, her grumbling not deterring him. What good was a challenge if it wasn't a challenge? "How about heading over to the Broken Spur after we drop off your suitcase and the fur ball?"

"You go." She sounded wary. "I'm tired. I think I'll just go to bed."

He glanced her way. She was staring forward, her brow beetled, her lower lip stuck out in a pout. She looked as if she was fighting with herself, so he opted to give it one more try. "I think you want to go."

She glanced at him, and the flash in her eyes had nothing to do with a passing streetlight. "Think again, cowboy. You go pollinate to your heart's content, but leave me out of it!"

Positive he'd heard wrong, he pulled to a stop at a red light and angled around to see her better. "Pollinate?"

She had shifted to stare out her window. At his query she faced him, her expression dismayed. "I—I said *party*. You go *party* to your heart's content. That's what I said."

He watched her closely. Even in the dimness he could see a shadow of embarrassment darken her face. She hadn't said party. She'd said pollinate. He ran a hand over his chin, wondering at that. What did she think he was, anyway? A damn bumblebee? Okay, maybe he liked women and they liked him. But he was pickier than she gave him credit for.

The stoplight changed to green, the color reflecting in her glasses. When he stepped on the gas, he came to the conclusion she'd had all the teasing she could cope with for one night. If she was so terrified that he wanted to put his stinger—or whatever it was bumblebees did the dirty with—between her petals, he would back off. "Okay, Miss Emerson. Whatever you want."

He had a notion she didn't know what she wanted. Or maybe she did, and it wasn't him. He felt bad about teasing her. She'd had a rough couple of days. He hadn't meant to come on to her tonight. But damn, she was a cute little oddball. When she'd put on his hat and bandanna, something inside him had gone haywire.

He'd suddenly wanted her.

It was the weirdest thing the way it hit him. And it hadn't worn off by the time he'd made that remark about hoping the panties in the freezer were hers. Sure, he'd thought kidding her was a good idea at the time. But it wasn't his brains that had been doing his thinking.

Now he realized he'd been an insensitive jerk. Miss Dee-dee Emerson wasn't emotionally ready for a roll in the hay. Maybe his first instinct yesterday had been right. Maybe she wasn't a player. He didn't run into many "commitment" die-hards. It would be damn hilarious to have one staying under the same roof. One of God's little jokes.

"Hell," he muttered.

"What?" He could hear her anxiety.

"Nothing." He eyed her soberly. Okay, so he wanted her, and he loved a challenge. But he wasn't into forced sex. Until he got some dead-bang let's-do-it-cowboy signals from her, he'd shift his libido into neutral.

He decided a subject change was in order. "Say, sugar, did I mention that was good apple pie?"

"I only peeled," she said, still sounding cautious.

"Sugar, you can peel for me any day." He glanced at her, noting her anxious frown. *Shoot.* What the hell was the matter with him? Hadn't he just promised himself no more teasing? Biting back a curse, he redoubled his vow to be a good boy. "So—how does it happen that somebody who can't cook writes the Winnie's Helpful Hints column?"

"Wrote," she corrected, looking morose.

"Right." He felt a twinge of guilt. *Great, Gentry, remind her she doesn't have a job.*

"Geez, that would have been a wonderful career." She slumped back, obviously emotionally drained. Garth figured she felt worse about losing that position than anything.

"You don't have to talk about it if it's too painful."

She laughed deep in her throat, the sound melancholy. "It's better than some subjects," she muttered.

Garth knew what she meant, and kept his mouth shut.

After a few minutes of silence, she sighed. "Well, first of all the Winnie's Helpful Hints column isn't about cooking." She ran her hands through her hair. "Actually, it was an emergency situation. I was doing obits at the time, but I'd become friends with the columnist, Bernie Katzmonger, and—"

"Bernie Katzmonger?" Garth asked with a chuckle. "A guy wrote the column?"

"Don't be a chauvinist," she admonished. "Giving household hints is *not* gender specific."

"Whoa, sugar." He squinted at her. "Don't get riled. I just figured you took over for some sweet old lady named Winnie."

"Well, I didn't. Bernie had been doing the column for six years, since the original Winnie retired." She cleared her throat and bent forward. Garth glanced her way as she reached inside the cage to stroke Magnolia's back. "Anyway…one day, Bernie phoned to ask me to cover for him and write his column. It's reader questions and answers. So I picked a couple of questions I could answer and did it.

What I couldn't answer, I got out of reference books we have at the paper.''

"Cheatin', huh?'' he kidded. The scowl on her face told him that was the wrong thing to say. Apparently her lack of a formal college education was a sore subject with her.

"No,'' she said with defiance. "I was *researching,* then using what I learned to instruct.''

Her face was pale, serious and proud. He took pity on her, sorry that he'd pushed one of her buttons. "And you did such an outstanding job, Bernie got the boot?''

"No,'' she said quietly. "Even after I'd been doing it for three weeks, nobody guessed. They thought he was writing the column from home. When he finally called to say he was quitting, he told the managing editor the truth and suggested they pass the job to me.''

Garth grinned. "I like him.''

That elicited the first near smile he'd seen this whole trip. "Me, too. Now he's doing real well performing as Countess Catsup at a local alternative life-style club.'' She paused, and Garth could feel her eyes on him. Clearly she expected him to make a remark. He'd be darned if he would. If she was going to get her dander up, she was going to have to do it alone. "Don't you have anything to say?'' she prodded thinly.

With his face absolutely straight, Garth glanced at her. "Sounds like he made an economically sound decision.''

"What is *that* supposed to mean?''

With a low chuckle, Garth shook his head. "I give up, sugar.'' He glanced away to watch traffic. "You want to fight with me so bad, you go right ahead.''

She was quiet for a long time. When he looked her way again, she was slouched against the seat, her eyes closed. "What, no fight?''

She rolled her head from side to side. "No—sorry." She glanced at him. "I guess I'm just on edge."

He pursed his lips, experiencing a stitch of compassion. She looked pretty wrung out. "How about a truce?" He smiled, making sure there was no trace of teasing in the expression.

She nodded. "Okay. You don't tease me and I won't snipe at you."

He held out his hand. "Shake."

She took it. She had strong, cool little hands. He'd watched them earlier that evening as she'd massaged the phone with alcohol. There had been a sensuality in her movements that aroused him. "Friends?" she asked.

After a couple of seconds, she pulled away and he grasped the wheel, trying to concentrate on the highway. *Okay,* he agreed silently. *Until you say different, sugar, I'll keep my hands to myself.*

"Yeah," he murmured. "Friends."

DEEDEE'S ROOM WAS PLAIN, but cozy. The bed's old springs squeaked every time she breathed, but the sheets were clean and the scarred dresser was roomy enough for her things.

The moon shone in the window, bright and nearly full, though on the wane. Sheers wagged and flapped in the night breeze. The quiet time of night had fallen, after the crickets quit droning and before the birds began to chirp. She'd turned off the air conditioner about midnight and opened the window. The cool breeze felt nice against her face.

Rolling to her side, she gazed at Magnolia, peacefully sleeping beside her. On her back, all fours splayed upward, Magnolia looked dead. Deedee smiled, stroking the ferret's belly. Somehow watching the contented little darling made Deedee feel less nervous.

Darn that Garth and his I-was-hoping-the-panties-were-yours remark. He'd almost given her a heart attack when he'd said that. Visions of uninhibited carnal acts had whizzed through her brain, and she'd had to struggle not to leap up and plant a kiss on those sexy, taunting lips.

The rapscallion knew what he was doing. No doubt he seduced lots of women that way—hoping erotic things about them out loud! *Oh, sugar, I was hoping that smell of cabbage was really you, 'cause it surely turns me on.* Deedee squeezed her eyes shut, trying not to think about him and his stupid, obvious lines. *Oh, sugar, I was hoping you'd sit down to dinner and take a bite of spinach. I've been fantasizing about it all day.* Geez, the man could turn anything into an erotic event. All he had to do was look at you with those bedroom eyes and drawl any foolish rot.

So why was she wasting her precious time thinking about him?

After all his talk about how it was a Saturday night and he wanted to go to the Dirty Sock, or whatever the dance hall was called, he hadn't ended up going. Even though she'd immediately escaped to her bedroom, unpacked and taken care of Magnolia, she hadn't heard his truck leave. And she'd listened.

When she'd come out of her room about eleven, to brush her teeth, she'd heard the shower running and realized Garth was getting ready for bed.

Wondering for the millionth time why he'd decided not to go out partying, she squinted at her wristwatch. It was just after three. She groaned, muttering, "I'll be one fine, puffy-eyed specimen in the morning."

*Sugar, I was hopin' you wouldn't get any sleep. Those puffy eyes make me hot.* She winced, running a hand over her face. "Enough already!" This mental nonsense couldn't go on or she'd never get any rest.

Glancing at Magnolia, she made a quick decision. Scooping up her pet, she whisked it into its cage, gently placing her into her hammock. The little sweetie didn't even stir. That was one odd quirk about ferrets. When they were sound asleep, they were practically comatose.

The T-shirt Deedee had worn to bed came almost to her knees, so she decided she was decent enough for hoot owls and possums. Slipping on her glasses and a pair of scuffs, she picked her way downstairs. As she tiptoed though the dark living room toward the door, the swing at one end of the porch seemed to beckon to her.

She'd spent many nights sitting on the porch swing at her daddy's place. That had been one of the few things she'd enjoyed during her childhood—swinging and dozing, letting the day's strains and hurts drift from her mind and heart. Maybe the soft motion of the swing would lull her into drowsiness, and she could go back upstairs and fall asleep.

Without a sound, she opened the front door and tiptoed to the wooden swing at the far side of the porch, where the moonlight peeked in. Sitting down at one end, she pushed off with her feet, then lifted her legs so that she could curl up. Resting her head against one armrest, she settled her feet on the other.

The chain squeaked each time she swung forward, but the sound was pleasant, nostalgic. Her porch swing had squeaked exactly the same way. Maybe it was a law that all porch swings had to squeak.

She gazed at the stars. The night was clear, free of clouds. The breeze blew softly, caressing her hair. As she swept a strand out of her face, she inhaled, enjoying the sweet night scents of summer.

The squeaks came closer and closer together as the swing lost momentum. "I need somebody to push me," she mumbled, uncurling herself to give the swing another jump start.

"Will I do?" asked a voice from the shadows at the other end of the porch.

The disembodied question startled Deedee so badly, she had to grab the chain to keep from tumbling off head first. Her glasses weren't so lucky. They dropped to the floorboards with a clatter. Then utter silence reigned.

She wanted to die and blow away like dust. Garth lurked somewhere in the darkness. He'd been watching her!

"You okay?" he asked, and this time Deedee heard the creak of wood as he approached. But she heard no sound of boots.

Swallowing, she found her voice. "I—I'm okay, but I'm not sure about my glasses."

He appeared in the dimness and, vague and blurry though he was, her heart did a stupid little flip-flop. He wasn't wearing a shirt, but thankfully wore jeans. She glanced down and, though she couldn't be sure, decided he must be barefoot. "What are you doing out here?" she asked, unable to keep a flutter of unease from her voice.

"I was about to ask you the same question."

He loomed before her now, all soft-focus male contours in the moonlight. He bent and she squinted, trying to follow what he was doing. Unfortunately her glance caught on his marvelous back—even more erotic under a golden moon—and she forgot everything else.

"Here they are," he said.

She jerked up, befuddled. "What?"

He held out a blurry object. "Your glasses."

"Oh." She felt like a dimwit. Grabbing them, she slid them on, grateful to find they were no worse for their little sky dive. "Uh—thanks."

His half grin was lazy, troubling. "No problem." He straightened and moved around to the back of the swing. "You curl up like you were. I'll push."

Her cheeks sizzled with mortification. "What were you going to do, stay over there in the dark and spy on me?"

He pushed and she swung forward, but she was no longer in the mood for quiet contemplation of the night sky. Shifting around, she lay an arm across the back of the swing and glared. "*Were* you?"

He pushed again, his teeth flashing, setting her heart into a disturbing series of high kicks. "Look at it from my side, sugar," he said. "If you were out on the porch in the middle of the night and somebody else showed up, what would you look at?"

She couldn't argue with his blasted logic. "I would have *said* something," she insisted.

"I did."

"I've been out here five minutes."

He pushed again, but eleven whole squeaks came and went and he still hadn't responded. After the twelfth, she couldn't stand it one instant longer. "Aren't you going to say *anything?*"

He shrugged. In the moonlight the dynamic shifting of muscles made a gratifying show. "You told me once there was this place between the truth and a lie where you keep your mouth shut. Remember?"

She frowned. "So?"

"So, sugar, you won't like the truth, and I don't like to lie."

Something tingled in the pit of her stomach. She didn't know what it was or why, and she wasn't sure she'd like the answer if somebody told her. But for some absurd reason she had to know what he *wasn't* saying. "Oh, for Pete's sake, Garth. I survived the frozen panties remark, so I can survive this.''

''Okay.'' He half nodded, not looking convinced by her bravado. ''The truth is, Deedee, I thought if I made myself known we'd end up doing more than talking. I don't figure that's what you want—quite yet.''

Her mouth sagged open. *Well, you insisted that he say something,* her brain scolded. ''More than talking?'' she breathed, her mouth disconnecting itself from her good sense.

He nodded, pushing the swing again. ''Yeah.''

''Like what?'' she heard herself whisper, afraid she already knew the answer, but needing to hear it from his own lips.

''Sugar...'' He cocked his head, clearly dubious. ''*You* know like what.''

She lifted her chin, shaking her head. Something unruly within her wasn't going to let him get away with that non-answer. ''No. Like what, Garth?''

She watched his brow furrow. With both fists, he gripped the back of the swing, bringing it to a halt. She grabbed on, her hand covering one of his. ''I'd kiss you,'' he said quietly.

She couldn't seem to remove her hand from his, and just stared. ''You would?''

''Yeah.'' His head dipped toward her.

''What kind of a kiss?'' Her common sense was tapping her on the mental shoulder, shrieking something about asking for trouble, but she paid no heed.

''It wouldn't be on your cheek.'' He slid her glasses off and pocketed them.

''No?'' Her body quivered. She liked the idea of Garth not kissing her on her cheek.

''And it wouldn't be brotherly.''

"Wouldn't?" Even better. She didn't want a brother. *But you don't want a one-night stand, either, Deedee!* her brain counseled desperately. *He's just interested in pollinating! Don't be a stupid flower! You'll get all emotionally involved and he'll have forgotten your name by the end of the week!*

He drew very near, close enough that his breath teased her lips. "We'd end up all naked and sweaty."

"We would?" She'd seen him sweaty and she'd liked what she saw. But naked? Did she dare? *Deedee,* her brain yelled, *If pollinating were against the law, Garth Gentry's mug shot would be in every post office in America! Don't do this! You'll feel like yesterday's newspaper when the dawn comes!*

His lips hovered. "It's now or never, sugar," he murmured, sounding very, very into the idea of "now." She was the only one left who might still say no. But she didn't want to say no. Now or never meant *now!*

Her lips parted to accept his kiss, and it was the instant his mouth touched hers that her brain finally assimilated the meaning of "now or never." It meant *I'm hot to pollinate you, baby, but don't expect a Christmas card.* That's what "now or never" meant! Tonight—then never again.

Feeling as though she'd been stung, she jerked away from the fledgling caress of his lips. "Oh, lord!" she cried. Hopping off the swing, she stumbled away to a safe distance. She held out a hand. "Give me my glasses and don't come out from behind that swing!"

He remained bent forward, his fists curled over the back of the swing. His jaw tensed visibly. Dark hair tousled by the breeze blew into his eyes and he brushed it away, then replaced the hand on the swing as though he needed support. "Hell, sugar," he groused, "give me a minute." Several heartbeats later, he cleared his throat, finally straightening to look at her. His dusky features were unsmiling.

She reiterated her demand for the return of her glasses by stiffening her arm and spreading her fingers wider.

"Okay, okay." He tugged her eyeglasses from his pocket and held them out. "You caught me. This whole seduction thing was a plot to steal your specs."

She snatched them, taking care not to touch his hand. Her mouth was giving her fits, tingling from the brief contact with his. It wasn't fair to have lips that were such traitors. What had she ever done to make the sensitive little expanses of flesh hate her that way?

She licked her lips, wanting to wipe away the sensation. It didn't work. If she ever actually let him kiss her—full mouth-to-mouth contact—she would be lost! *Blam!* Pollinated before she knew what was happening. She sucked in a long breath, trying to feel relief that she'd found out in time.

Planting her glasses on her face, she shoved them high on her nose, wincing at the pain she caused herself. If she didn't have two black eyes in the morning it would be a miracle.

Movement caught her eye and she stiffened. "Don't!"

He'd started to walk around the swing, but stopped. "Sugar, I'd like to sit down." He lifted his hands in a show of surrender. "Do you mind?"

She gritted her teeth. "I don't trust you."

He kept his hands up, as though under arrest. "I know what no means. I'm not going to jump you."

*Darn!*

*No—no, I don't mean that!* her brain backpedaled, fighting for control over her craving. She watched him move to the front of the swing and drop down. Leaning back, he peered at her through narrowed eyes. "So do you still want to swing?'' He crossed his arms over his chest, apparently indicating he wouldn't touch her.

She mirrored his movement, crossing her own arms. ''I'm out of the mood.''

He grinned, but it was a mockery of a smile. ''Wish *I* could say that.''

A shiver ran up her spine. She only wished her body's reaction indicated revulsion. She wondered if he realized how the moon paid tribute to his physique—long, lean and tempting in the soft light. His muscles rippled at the slightest movement.

He was tall enough to reach the floor flat-footed, so he began to swing back and forth, back and forth, not very far, for his feet remained squarely on the floor. The swing squeaked out a rhythm that squawked with every fourth thud of her heart. She wondered if he could hear the accompaniment being belted out in her chest.

''You're in my way, sugar,'' he said at last.

She jumped, never thinking he was restricting his swinging to keep from bashing her in the thighs. ''Oh!'' She sidestepped clumsily.

''You can still swing. I'll push.'' He said it matter-of-factly. Apparently he'd managed to get out of the mood, after all. ''Come on, Deedee,'' he coaxed. ''That's what you came out here for. I'll be a gentleman.'' He winked, making her feel all warm and mushy. ''Honest.''

She lifted her chin. Any sensible woman would have turned tail and run into the house, thanking heaven she'd made it safely away with her pride intact and her clothes not scattered in the trees. But no, Deedee Emerson was actually moving toward the swing.

*Dingbat!* her brain complained as she sat down. Lifting her feet to the seat, she pulled her big T-shirt over her knees, stuffing the hem under her scuffs. Now, she was little more than a lump with a head.

"Cold?" He sounded amused at her turtle act.

She grasped the chain, staring straight ahead. "Just push."

# 5

THE SOUND OF HUMMING jarred Deedee out of her guarded contemplation. She jerked to look at Garth. His gaze shifted her way when she stirred. He was resting an elbow on the armrest, his fist propped under his nose. She saw a crooked smile appear around that fist, but he kept humming. The song was country, and that didn't surprise her. What other kind of music would a cowboy hum?

She didn't recognize the tune. It was just something sultry and sexy that had climbed high enough on the charts for her to have heard it once or twice. She eyed him with misgiving as he watched her. Deedee reluctantly admitted he had a nice hum. The tempo fitting his rocking, the tune flowed from his throat, deep and mellow. She didn't think that other Garth—the famous one—could have done much better with his sound stage, professional band and backup singers.

Swallowing, she turned away. She'd be darned if she'd ask him the name of the tune. Knowing that taunting grin, it probably had a name like "Let's Have Sex All Night" or something equally erotic. What was she doing out here, anyway?

"Do you recognize that song?" he asked.

She shook her head, chewing on her lip.

He grinned that annoying, sexy grin. Glancing away, he began to hum again.

After a time, to her amazement, she found herself relaxing. His soft humming was simply too melodious not to have a calming effect. And the swing weaved its restful spell, even though The Pollinator was doing the swinging. She leaned back. Closing her eyes, she allowed the beauty of the tune and the resonance of Garth's voice to wash over her with the night breeze....

Deedee woke with a start. How had she allowed herself to fall asleep out here on the swing, next to Garth?

As she scrambled to sit up, she heard the squawk of what sounded like bedsprings. Her eyes flew open, all manner of sex-riddled scenarios flashing through her mind. What had happened? How had she gotten into bed? Her hands flew to her mouth, covering a gasp. Had Garth carried her to his...

Blinking, she looked around, frowning in confusion. If he had carried her to his bed, then his room looked exactly like hers. Even blurry. And he'd moved Magnolia into his room, too. Deedee scooted up to sit and shook her head, trying to clear it. How in the world had she gotten here?

She cast around for her glasses, then spotted them on the bedside table, right where she usually left them. Once she'd planted them on her face, she squinted at the windup clock. Seven-thirty. Still bewildered, she peered down at herself. She wasn't even the slightest bit naked.

Had she sleepwalked back to bed? She cringed as a fledgling thought tried to burrow into her brain, but she wouldn't allow it. *No.* She would not believe that Garth had carried her up here. Absolutely not! That was not an option. Garth Gentry didn't carry women to bed and tuck them in like they were three years old. That wasn't the sort of man he was. Even his grandmother knew that.

Deedee felt restless and cranky, hating the way her heart hammered. Why was she irritated at the possibility that Garth Gentry had scooped her up, limp and—if her luck was running true to form—snoring? Then he'd carried her to her bed and—and—left her there. Alone!

"Deedee, you will not be insulted. You will be grateful. The man behaved like a gentleman," she muttered. "He said he would, didn't he?"

She sat there scowling, her hands working in her lap. Finally logic won out and she realized she'd skimmed out of *that* one. In the clear light of day, she could see that Garth might be sexy and gorgeous, but he was hardly a fountainhead of security. He took nothing seriously—not women, not sex, not love. Besides, he was a cowboy.

She had to keep a tight grip on her goal. She was looking for the forever brand of love. Not only that, she wanted the financial security her dad had never been able to give her. Maybe that's why she'd been so blindly attracted to Tyler. He represented financial security on a princely scale.

Unlike Garth, who represented fun and games and an adios-sugar-have-a-good-life morality. Unfortunately, he also represented sexual gratification on a princely scale. Her body involuntarily warmed with the memory of their almost kiss, and she sucked in air to clear her mind.

She must not allow thoughts of the man to mess with her head. A relationship with him would be about as workable as trying to dry feather pillows in a dryer without adding a pair of tennis shoes. Unthinkable. She needed both "tennis shoes"—security and that eternal kind of love—to find happiness with a man.

A tap-tap on her door brought her head up with a start. "Yes?"

"You awake?"

Garth's voice had an unsettling effect, and the deep gulp of air she'd just taken left her in a rush. "Uh…"

He laughed. "I'll take that as a yes. Breakfast is ready."

She experienced a surge of guilt. She was supposed to

be helping with breakfast. "Why didn't my alarm go off?" she cried.

"I turned it off, sugar," he said. "You were as dead as a can of corned beef last night."

She squeezed her eyes shut, embarrassed. She stuck her fingers under her glasses and rubbed her eyes. "Corned beef," she muttered. An imp in her brain wheedled, *Sugar, I was hoping you wouldn't remind me of corned beef, 'cause that's the only thing that turns me off.*

"You say something?"

She shuddered. "I'll be right there."

"You're not upset that I carried you up here, are you?"

She pulled her lips between her teeth in order to keep from screaming.

"Deedee?"

She couldn't stand it any longer and bounded out of bed, stalking to the door. Flinging it open was a bad mistake. He looked good enough to eat, lounging there all sexy male animal, a shoulder against the jamb. He wore tight jeans and a pure white T-shirt that didn't leave much about his torso to the imagination. "I..." Her mouth was suddenly dry. She couldn't remember what she'd been about to say. The only thing that came to mind was *Wow!* Bad idea, considering her goal was *not* to find this guy attractive. "Uh, I, uh..." She wondered if it would be her fate to remain frozen there, grunting out monosyllables for the rest of her life.

"Thank you, Garth?" he supplied, amusement twinkling in his eyes.

She swallowed, trying to soothe her throat. "Uh, right—I'll be down in a sec." Clamping her mouth shut, she slammed the door in his grinning face.

"My pleasure, sugar," he said softly through the door. "Don't give it another thought."

The sound of his boots faded as he went downstairs. Sagging against the door, she moaned, "I'm trying!"

DEEDEE FELT LIKE a world-class shirker, so to atone for not helping with breakfast, she decided she'd do something nobody on a ranch liked to do. Clara was taking a nap and Perry had just come in, complaining of the heat. After he clomped upstairs to join his wife in an afternoon siesta, Deedee left the house. Determined to do the right thing, she headed for the barn. She'd muck out the darned stalls, no matter how much she detested the chore. That would teach her to stay up until all hours having stupid fantasies about tight-tushed cowboys who thought of her as corned beef.

One of the double doors was open, and as she walked inside she was immediately hit by the familiar smells of musty animals and the earthy tang of rotting hay and dirt. She clenched her jaw. Okay, so she'd promised herself she'd never enter a barn again. So what? Poverty and homelessness had a way of changing one's priorities. She checked around, looking for the two-wheeled cart used for mucking out stalls. When she spotted it, she trudged over, scooping up a nearby pitchfork on the way. She hauled the cart to the first stall.

"What do you think you're doing?"

She whirled to see Garth standing at the door of what must have been the tack room. He held a half-braided headstall. He didn't look any less sexy than he had this morning and that irked her no end. Needing to put emotional distance between them, she decided to be sarcastic. "I'm Cinderella on my way to the ball." With a sweet smile she propped a jogging shoe on the edge of the cart. "Like my glass slippers?"

He turned toward the tack room, tossing the headstall

inside. When he faced her again, he strolled her way. "I'll do that. I'm picky about how it's done."

She took her foot off the cart and made a dubious face. "It doesn't exactly take a rocket scientist to muck out a stall."

He came up to her, tall, broad-shouldered, adding his delicious scent to the mix. "You go on back to the house." He took the pitchfork from her hand.

"I've mucked out lots of stalls in my day." She grabbed for the tool, but he moved it out of reach.

"Nope."

Exasperated, she snatched the pitchfork and yanked. "Give me that!" When he let go, she almost fell on her backside. Righting herself, she brushed hair out of her face. "Thanks," she snapped.

His grin was wry. "I'm not going to fight you for it, sugar. You want to muck up horse hockey so bad, go for it. I was just trying to be a gentleman."

"Well, don't." She snatched the cart's handles and unlatched the stall door. Just then a wasp whizzed out, skimming by her face. She instinctively dodged, waving it off. Spinning, she could only watch helplessly as it landed on Garth's cheek.

"Hell," he yelped, swatting it away.

"Did it sting you?" His wince was answer enough. "Don't move," she cried. "I'll be right back!"

Not more than a minute later she returned from the house, a thick slice of onion in her hand. "Hold still." Panting, she slapped it on the sting, then took a piece of duct tape and secured it to his skin.

"What in thunder..." He stared at her as though he'd just seen her flap her arms and crow like a rooster.

He reached up but she grasped his wrist. "No, leave it. Onion draws out the poison."

He frowned, then blinked. His earthy eyes began to glisten. "It's making me blind, sugar."

She held on to his wrist. It was a large wrist connected to a very strong arm. She knew if he was absolutely resolved to remove the onion she would be laughably unequal to stopping him, unless maybe she leaped up and mounted his elbow. Then she'd have the other arm to deal with.

A tear slid from one stunning brown eye and those long, lush lashes blinked again. He reached into his hip pocket and pulled out a green bandanna. "This is stupid," he grumbled.

"No, you'll thank me. How does it feel?"

His half grin was mocking. "Like I have an onion taped to my face." He wiped his cheek. "How long does this take?"

"Five minutes." That was the absolute minimum, but she figured he wouldn't hold still any longer. "It'll be worth it." She could feel his arm relax, so she let go. That was a good thing because her fingers were registering his skin, the torque of muscle and the silky feel of wrist hair with far too much intensity.

He closed his eyes, pinching the bridge of his nose. "This is nuts."

She had to smile. He was cute when he was being blinded by onion fumes. "You're very brave," she teased.

He squinted at her. "I take it back, we can make stall mucking one of your regular chores."

"What's going on here?" It was Perry's unmistakable bellow.

Deedee turned to see the elderly man outlined in the barn door. "Garth got stung by a wasp."

"Huh?" Perry tramped toward them. "Garth, boy, what you got stuck to your head?"

Garth chuckled deep in his throat and Deedee was struck

by the beauty of his glittering brown eyes, filled with tears and laughter. "Hi, Grandpa." Pointing to the onion slice, he said, "Snack. I'm saving it for later."

Deedee couldn't help but giggle.

He wiped at his eyes with the bandanna, then lounged against the stall.

When Perry got close, he squinted at the onion, lifted his glasses off his nose and got close enough to sniff. "Wheeoo, boy, that's an onion."

"It's a wasp-sting remedy," Deedee yelled, drawing Perry's amazed attention.

The older man replaced the glasses on his face. "You don't say?" He shook his head. "Cure looks worse than the disease. Stinks worse, for sure."

Deedee grinned, fairly certain Garth agreed. "Why aren't you taking a nap?"

"Nap?" Perry asked and Deedee nodded. "Couldn't sleep with that old woman snoring fit to shake ticks out of the weeds. Thought I'd come out and visit with the boy." He eyed his grandson. "But if you're gonna smell like—"

"I'm done," Garth interrupted, pulling off the onion poultice. He startled Deedee by leaning her way, the injured cheek at eye level. "How am I?"

She examined his profile for blemishes and came up empty, deciding a wasp sting would do little to mar such a happy combination of features. His lips were just full enough for kissing, his lashes to die for, and those lusty brown eyes...

"Bad?" he asked, glancing her way. Their lips were suddenly very close.

She started, not realizing she'd been woolgathering about the man's face. "Uh—no, not at all." She smiled weakly and took a protective backward step. "There's not even a red mark."

He tossed the onion slice into the cart. "Shoulda told you, sugar. Wasp stings don't affect me much."

Her buoyant mood disappeared. "Oh…"

"But…" His voice drew her gaze back to his face. He touched his cheek, rubbing as though testing a good shave. "I don't know when my skin's been this smooth." His wink was charming and playful.

Encircling Perry's slumped shoulders with an arm, he aimed his grandfather toward the tack room, but his attention remained on Deedee. She couldn't help but be tickled by his absurd remark. Clearly he'd been trying to make her feel better, and she felt a thrill of gratitude. Her light-hearted mood returned and she grinned. "I bet your tear ducts have never been cleaner, either."

As Garth led his grandfather away, his laughter filled the air. Deedee's pulse leaped at the strength and warmth of the sound.

Somehow, barns didn't seem all that grim at the moment.

GARTH LAY IN BED, his hands supporting his head as he stared at the ceiling. Lips twitching with amusement, he recalled almost tripping over Deedee this afternoon while she was dusting talcum powder in a crack between planks in the parlor's oak floor. With big, serious eyes she'd told him she was getting rid of a squeak. And by heaven, that spot didn't squeak after her talcum treatment.

These past six days with Little Miss Helpful Hints in the house had been interesting. She'd used up one whole container of shaving cream to clean Perry's easy chair. No matter how nuts it seemed, Garth had to admit the old chair looked better. He chuckled. Deedee Emerson was one strange case. But she was trying hard to be helpful.

He closed his eyes only to see her cute, serious face and those big, soulful eyes. "Turn around, sugar," he mumbled. "Let's see that nicely rounded little tail." He opened his eyes. Damnation. The woman wouldn't even obey him in his fantasies. She just went on dribbling talcum on the floor or splinting broken house plant's limbs with toothpicks and tape.

The woman doggedly resisted getting naked for him—awake or asleep. And he knew she was interested. He'd sensed it that night on the porch swing. But she had no intention of giving in to her feelings.

He opened his eyes, irritated with himself for his preoccupation with Deedee Emerson. What in hell was his problem? This was not a cutting competition. She was not his competitor; she was a woman. And she didn't want to have sex with him. It didn't matter why, that was just the way it was. Why couldn't he leave it at that? All he had to do for willing female companionship was head over to the Broken Spur.

He closed his eyes again, vowing to get some sleep. Deedee didn't want to play, so he'd damn well better get his mind off her.

An odd noise at his door brought his eyes wide open. He listened, his gut clenching. *Let it be the little talcum-pourer-ivy-splinter.* He watched the doorknob in the darkness, cautiously optimistic. Usually his optimism got him everything he wanted, but he had grave doubts that Deedee would ever decide to see a sexual encounter with him as a good idea. Still, with the noise at the door, just maybe she wasn't as unfriendly to the idea as she acted. Maybe she simply wanted to make sure she was in control, that she could come and go as she pleased.

He peered at the door. The knob hadn't moved, but now he heard another noise. It sounded like skittering feet. An instant later, Garth felt light pressure on his chest and found himself staring into tiny eyes. He jerked involuntarily, lifting an arm to slam the thing into oblivion. But the split second before he made good on his intention, he realized what it was. He would bet the heart attack it almost gave him that this critter's eyes were burgundy. "Magnolia," he growled under his breath.

The ferret ventured farther up his chest to sniff his jaw. "Oh, fine." He eyed heaven, but for some reason found the idea of a ferret perched on his chest perfectly reasonable, considering whose pet this was. The irony of the situation struck him and he eyed the tiny beast with amusement. Magnolia took that opportunity to place her forepaws on his chin for a closer look at his face. "Apparently my mental telepathy needs work, Maggie, old girl," he mumbled. "I was signaling the *other* female in your room."

Magnolia startled him by scampering across his face onto his pillow. The next thing he knew there was a cold, damp nose in his ear, then the unmistakable flick of a curious little tongue. "Okay, that's it. Yours is not the tongue I wanted in my ear." He rose and picked up the four-legged flirt. "You're going back to your cage."

When he reached the door, he grew puzzled. It was closed. "How did you do that?"

Magnolia simply blinked at him.

"A woman of mystery, huh?" He shook his head. "Just don't do it again. What if Dawg had been in here? You'd have given him a stroke."

Outside Deedee's room, he hesitated. Her door was closed, too. He eyed the ferret. "Your name should be Houdini." He lifted his fist to knock, then stopped. It was four in the morning. He hadn't heard her bedsprings squeaking for hours. Flinching, he realized he'd spent most of the night listening as he made faulty attempts at fantasizing. *Hell.*

Resolving not to disturb her, he opened the door and

slipped inside. She'd made a point of explaining why she hadn't talcum powdered her bedroom floor; she'd said it could make Magnolia sick. Garth prayed there were no squeaking floorboards between the door and the ferret's cage. Lifting Magnolia to his face, he gave her a hard look. "Not a sound out of you, either," he mouthed.

The mercury light on the barn was far enough from the house not to be glaring, but it gave him the faint illumination he needed to locate the cage. Slipping Magnolia inside, he stealthily fastened the latch. Magnolia turned on him, chattering away.

He stood abruptly as though he'd been hit. Wincing, he jerked up his hands in a Stop signal, but realized the little traitor wouldn't know what the hell that meant. He glowered helplessly at the animal. All that damn noise would wake Deedee.

Worried, he peered at her. The second he did, her eyelids fluttered open. Her sleepy gaze passed over him and her eyes grew wide. She opened her mouth to scream, but his instincts gave him a head start and he practically fell on her to get his hand over her mouth.

"Don't yell, sugar." His harsh whisper sounded like a cannon shot in the quiet. "It's me." He fumbled for her glasses and, one-handed, managed to get them on her face. "See?"

Her gaze exhibited alarm and he hated that. She said something against his palm, but the pressure of his hand made it unintelligible. "This isn't what it looks like, sugar," he whispered. "I was returning Magnolia. She got into my room."

Deedee blinked and Garth watched as she fixed her eyes on the cage. Her ferret was inside, chattering and scampering back and forth, apparently enjoying the show. "She wasn't locked up when you went to sleep, was she?'' He tried to sound reasonable and unthreatening.

Deedee stared at him. The alarm in her eyes had diminished, but wasn't totally gone. "If you promise to be calm, I'll take my hand away."

She watched him for a few seconds before she nodded. He eyed her dubiously. "Promise?"

Her gaze narrowed to slits and she said something else, but it was muffled under his palm.

"What?"

She made a growling sound, as though frustrated. Slowly, he released his hand. "Okay, what?"

"I said, Garth, take your hand off of my mouth."

"Oh." He chuckled.

When he sat back, she glared at him. "You don't expect me to *believe* that story, do you?"

He shrugged. "Come on, sugar. Give me points for originality, at least."

"That's what I thought!" She sat up, looking as though she planned to jump out of bed and find something heavy to bop him with.

"Hush, sugar." He grasped her shoulders, pressing her down. "I was kidding! Calm down. I'd rather not have my grandmother know about this."

"You'd be surprised what your grandmother knows!" Deedee lay back, but remained stiff, her body language telling him she trusted him about as far as she could toss a horse. But she didn't appear quite so intent on leaping up and searching for a weapon, so he let go.

Her glance flicked to his bare chest and her eyes grew wide again. He could tell that from her vantage point she couldn't see below his waist. He shook his head. "I'm wearing shorts." He winked. "Don't want to make it too easy for you."

She shrank back into her pillow, dragging her sheet up to her neck. "I—I don't—that thought never..." She floundered for another second, her mouth working, before she pointed to the door. "Just go."

"Okay, okay." He started to get up, but caught sight of Magnolia, and his curiosity was rekindled. Gesturing toward the cage, he asked, "How the hell did she get into my room without opening any doors?"

Deedee stared at him, and he could see her swallow. "I hope you don't think I did it."

He ran a hand through his hair, trying not to be aggravated that she wasn't flirting and trailing a finger along his belly by now. "I know you didn't." He had no intention of getting into why he knew she hadn't. "But she got in. So how?"

Deedee peered at her ferret. "She can get under doors." Her attention flitted back to him. "I'm sorry if she woke you."

She was sorry she woke him! *Hell!* His exasperation swelled to irritation. "No problem," he drawled, mockery in his tone. "I've had females climb on top of me in the middle of the night before."

Her lips formed a stunned O at his risqué statement. He knew he shouldn't have said that, but he was tired and frustrated—and ticked off at her for *not* being a female who jumped on his chest. Her stiff-armed attitude was getting on his nerves. She sure knew how to puncture a man's ego. Deciding to pay her back just a little for his discomfort, he leaned forward, planting a hand on either side of her face.

With a quick dip of his head, he ran his tongue across her lips. Their eyes met for a fraction of a second. Intense physical awareness shot through him. Feeling as though he'd been burned—no, more like electrocuted—he pushed himself off her bed and lurched from her room.

Once outside, he began to feel like the jerk he was. What had come over him? He'd promised to keep his hands off her, but that probably should have included his tongue.

Cursing himself for a horny bastard, he rubbed his hand across his mouth. Biting back a raw curse, he vowed he'd go to the Broken Spur tomorrow night. He needed the companionship of some neighborly female whose lips weren't wired to kill.

# 6

DEEDEE DIDN'T SEE Garth all the next day. He was up and gone before she came down to help with breakfast. According to Clara, he'd gone into Tulsa to run some errands. Deedee heard his truck return after lunch, but he spent most of the afternoon in the tractor shed repairing the hay bailer. Deedee finished the dinner dishes before he came in to eat. By then, she'd gone to her room to play with Magnolia. She breathed a sigh of relief, having managed to avoid him completely—so far.

She was glad he'd made himself scarce, because she was still rattled by the surprise tongue thing last night. After he'd left her room, she was afraid she'd died, for she stopped breathing. It took a lot of painful concentration to get started again. Very deliberately she breathed in, out, in, out, in, out....

Garth Gentry was a cruel man. She'd never felt so aroused by a touch that lasted no longer than a split second. And the taste! Testosterone and toothpaste. Just thinking about the combination made her tingle all the way to her toes. She was afraid she would never be able to look at another tube of toothpaste again without experiencing a rush of desire. The man sure knew how to use his tongue!

She grasped her coffee cup with both hands and closed her eyes. Every time she thought about Garth and his darn tongue she got all weak and silly.

"Anything wrong, Deedee?" Clara asked, drawing her

back with the overloud question. "Don't you like *Unsolved Mysteries?*" She had to holler, because Perry was leaning toward the TV in his newly cleaned easy chair listening intently to the latest lost love segment. The TV blared loudly enough to locate those lost loves all by itself.

With a weak smile, Deedee faced the older woman. "No," she shouted, then bit her lip. That wasn't true. Where was her mind? "I mean yes, I enjoy the show."

Clara took the cup from her hand and set it on the coffee table. "This isn't any way for a healthy young woman to spend a Friday night. You need to have some fun. You've been cooped up here for a solid week working yourself to the bone."

Deedee heard the thud of Garth's boots as he came bounding down the stairs. "You're just the man I wanted to see," Clara called out.

Garth had taken his Stetson off the coatrack before he peered around the stairs. "Did you say something, Grandma?"

She waved him in. "Where are you going, boy?"

His glance flashed to Deedee before he focused on his grandmother. "I thought I'd run over to the Broken Spur for—"

"Nifty idea." Clara clapped her hands. "Take Deedee with you. She's looking a little peaked."

"Oh, no…" Deedee cried, knowing she would only get in the way of Garth's pollinating plans.

"Shush now, girl." Clara poked her shoulder. "Garth would be happy to have a pretty thing like you on his arm." She eyed him. "Wouldn't you, son?"

Deedee knew the older woman wasn't giving her grandson any choice and decided she'd better come down with a headache, fast. "I—I really don't think—"

Clara clutched Deedee's arm, hoisting her up. "She's

crazy about the idea, boy." The older woman's arthritic fingers could get a pretty fair grip when they wanted to. "You young folks go on and have a grand time."

Garth's half smile was almost convincing, but not quite. He held out a hand. "Come on, sugar. There's no fighting city hall."

Deedee couldn't see his eyes clearly beneath the shadow of his hat, but she had a feeling they weren't sparkling with delight. When she didn't move, he ambled forward and took her fingers. "Can you two-step?"

She shook her head.

"No problem. I can teach you."

She'd just bet he could. Gritting her teeth, she wished her mind didn't rush to visions of other things the man could teach her.

He'd tugged her onto the front porch before she realized what she was wearing. "But…these baggy jeans." Skidding to a halt, she picked at the big, old denim shirt she'd put on for comfort, not fashion. "I'm not dressed for going out." She studied Garth morosely. He was wearing freshly pressed jeans. His western shirt, with Native American symbols in earth tones, emphasized his tan skin and brown eyes. He looked yummy. She felt tacky.

His gaze roved over her. When their eyes met again, he pursed his lips. "Sugar," he said at last, "if you were my sister, that's exactly what I'd want you to wear." His slow grin was taunting. "Except maybe for the jogging shoes."

She frowned. What did that mean? No doubt she looked about as sexless as a man could hope for in a woman he didn't plan to get into a bar fight over. There was probably something to be said for honesty, but she couldn't think of it right now. "Thanks," she muttered as he led her down the front steps.

One tense minute later, she was beside him in his truck

and they were headed down the gravel drive. His expression was somber.

"I'm sorry about this," she said, meaning it. She could tell he was no happier about her tagging along than she was about going.

He slanted a glance her way. "I returned that ring today."

She was shocked. She'd completely forgotten about it. "Really?"

He turned to watch the road. "Gave it to Daddy De-Winter himself, down at the paper."

A tremor of apprehension slid through her. "Did he say anything?"

Garth pursed his lips. "A few things, but you don't want to hear them."

She sagged in the seat, fairly sure she knew. No doubt it was something about never darkening Tulsa's door again with the mistaken idea she'd get a job there. "Well, thanks for taking it back, anyway." She peered at him. "Did he want to know how you got it?"

Garth eyed her, his grin twisted. "Nope. Just peeled off five one-hundred-dollar bills and handed them to me." He shook his head, shifting to scan the road. "I think it would have been okay with him if I'd robbed you and left you in a ditch."

She sat forward. "He gave you five hundred dollars?"

"A reward."

She gaped, horrified. "And you took it?"

He chuckled. "Hold on, sugar. The money's on your dresser. I figured you might need some ready cash."

She frowned, suddenly upset but not sure why. "Okay, I'll leave. First thing in the morning."

He was wheeling his truck into the parking lot of a long low wooden building. A huge neon sign proclaimed the place to be The Broken Spur. Though the lot was packed, Garth drove up to the front door. To Deedee's surprise there was an open spot. He pulled in, then looked at her. "Hold on there," he said, his expression hard. "Nobody ever said you had to leave."

He reached behind the seat and grabbed his hat. "Thunderation, woman, you go off half-cocked more often than any female I've ever met." He climbed out and slammed his door. It surprised her when he came around and opened hers. "It's starting-over money, for whenever you feel like goin'. Now let's forget about it and dance." He took her hand and helped her down.

She stepped out of the truck, practically in front of the door. Wondering if it could possibly just be luck, she asked, "Do they keep a spot with your name on it?"

He glanced at her, plainly confused by the change of subject. "What?"

She waved at his truck. "How did you get such a good parking place?"

His chin came up in a half nod of understanding. "Oh." He shrugged. "You'd be surprised how many folks figure there won't be a spot up close, so they don't try." He winked. "I try, sugar. You'd be amazed how often a little extra tryin' works."

She looked up into those deadly sexy eyes and her heart lurched. She wouldn't be at all surprised. Not with this guy. That lick across her lips last night had told her exactly that about Garth Gentry. He didn't have a problem with giving things a try—be it finding a parking spot or finding a bed partner. She swallowed hard. If he tried much longer with her—licking and winking and touching—well, she had a feeling she might just open him up a spot. She kicked herself mentally. *No, Deedee! Don't even think like that!*

Her mind scrambled to think other, less erotic thoughts

and stumbled back to the topic of the DeWinters. When Garth grasped her elbow, she frowned at his profile. "I don't want starting-over money from Tyler's daddy," she insisted, deciding even an argument was better than thinking about Garth's sexual magnetism.

He squinted at her. "The money doesn't care where it comes from."

"I do."

He opened the cowboy club's door and aimed her inside. She was hit with a blast of jukebox music so loud it almost took away her breath. "Don't let pride make you stupid," he shouted.

Irked by his hard-nosed attitude, she yanked her arm from his grip. "So now I'm stupid?"

He leaned close and she got a pleasant whiff of his fresh-from-the-shower aroma. "You're not stupid. You're just too proud for your britches." He took her arm again, guiding her toward the postage-stamp-size tables. "Say, sugar, do you know how to get beer stains out of clothes?"

She was taken aback by his unexpected question. Still glaring at him, she nodded. "Sure."

His grin was disturbing. "Trust me. Keep it to yourself."

She sent him a black look. Clearly he had no intention of discussing the five hundred dollars any further. He'd accepted it. He'd given it to her. Subject closed. She inhaled to bring her temper under control. Even if she wanted to fight, wanted to shout at him, he would hardly notice. You had to shout in here just to be heard.

He found a table and motioned for her to sit. Before he could take his own seat, a pretty blonde hugged him with a squeal of delight. As the woman bounced up and down, Deedee noticed she was wearing jeans so tight the outline of a mole was visible on her thigh. Apparently unaware that Garth wasn't alone, the blonde took both of his hands and hauled him onto the dance floor. Deedee had a feeling this was just the tip of the iceberg of how tonight was going to go.

She absently picked at the complimentary bowl of popcorn on her table, eyeing him and his curvy partner as they slithered around the dance floor. You couldn't have gotten a straw between them. The woman wrapped both arms around his neck and glued her hips against his. She nuzzled his neck, and Deedee had a feeling her lips were doing things to him that didn't have anything to do with the two-step—if that's what the dance was supposed to be. It looked more like vertical sex.

Garth could certainly move. Though his dancing was subtle, it reeked with male sensuality. He was clearly a man who knew how to use his body and could use it to a woman's best advantage, if the blonde's possessiveness was any clue. And his grin, when he looked down into the woman's eyes, oozed raw sex. Deedee swallowed, startled to discover that her throat had gone dusty dry. What was she doing here?

"Can I get you something, hon?"

She forced her gaze away from Garth to look at the waitress, who was dressed in tight jeans and a brightly colored shirt, like almost everybody else in the place. The cowboy uniform. She remembered it well. The only feature on this waitress that made her look different than the patrons was the tray she carried. "Uh—well..." Deedee pushed her glasses more firmly into place. "A cola?"

The woman wrote it on a pad. "Diet? Regular?"

"Regular, I guess...."

"You alone?"

Deedee didn't know what to say, but shook her head. She didn't have a dime on her, so she hoped she wasn't alone. "I came with Garth Gentry." She raised a hand to point him out, but the look on the waitress's face made it clear she knew who he was. "Garth's here?" Her bored expression changed to animation and she stretched tall to inspect the room. Deedee couldn't see him anymore, but hoped he was still somewhere in the crush of dancers and not in the back seat of a car, licking....

She shook off the thought, telling herself sharply that who and what he licked was no concern of hers. She faced the waitress, trying to appear nonchalant. "I—I don't know what Garth wants—"

"I do, hon," the waitress interrupted, with a lurid grin. "The usual for Big Boy." She scribbled, disappearing into the rowdy throng.

Deedee sat there, staring at her hands as the blood drained from her face. *Big Boy!* She didn't even want to go there. Nicknames waitresses gave Garth Gentry did not affect her in the slightest.

Two more songs came and went without the waitress returning. Deedee munched absently on the popcorn, trying not to think about why she couldn't see Garth. Several cowboys had come by and asked her to dance, but she'd refused. She didn't know how to do these dances because she'd never had free time as a girl. And she didn't feel like making a fool of herself. Although, if she were to admit what she truly felt, it was depression. She didn't want to be here, witnessing how long Garth could stay out in some blonde's car doing the horizontal two-step before he had to come back and baby-sit her.

"Hi." She almost fell out of her chair in surprise when he appeared before her. This time a buxom little brunette was on his arm. "Inez, this is a houseguest of my grandparents, Deedee. Deedee, Inez."

The short woman gave Deedee the once-over and smiled the saccharine smile of a rival. "Hello," she said.

Deedee tried hard to make hers genuine. "Hi."

"Well," Garth said, giving Miss Busty a squeeze. "See you later, darlin'?"

Inez took his face in both her hands and drew him down, kissing him square on the mouth. "You call, now, Garth."

"Sure thing." His grin could have melted steel. Taking hold of his chair, he spun it around so he could straddle it. When the little brunette wiggled off, he folded his arms over the chair back. Deedee mused that he couldn't have placed himself any farther from her and still been at the same table.

He scanned the tiny tabletop. "Did you order something to drink?"

Deedee shrugged. "I thought so. Maybe the waitress got trampled."

He laughed, and even in the clamor, she could hear the richness of it. She crossed her legs, wondering why she felt the need.

"Hi, Garth!" called a feminine voice. Deedee had a hard time keeping annoyance from her expression. She had a feeling she'd be eating a lot of popcorn while she watched Garth dance with other women. When she turned, however, she was somewhat relieved to see the waitress standing there.

"Hi, darlin'." Garth grinned that melting grin. "What have you got for me?"

Even in the dimness Deedee could see the waitress blush. "Anything you want, honey. You know that." She set a cola in front of Deedee, then slid another tumbler in front of Garth. It was eerie how she couldn't manage to serve him without rubbing her chest against his arm. "Your usual." She bent further, whispering something in his ear. He sat back and laughed as he drew out a few bills. "Marry me, darlin'?"

Deedee was startled by the question, but the waitress playfully slapped his cheek as though she'd heard it before. "I'm all packed, you sweet thing."

When she was gone, Garth took a sip of his drink. Deedee watched him, then eyed the frosty glass. Maybe she'd heard the waitress wrong, before. Maybe the drink—his usual—was *called* a Big Boy. That was probably it. Though his glass wasn't any bigger than her own.

She took a gulp of her cola, trying to figure out what a drink called the Big Boy might have in it. His beverage was lighter than her cola. So, maybe a Big Boy was ninety percent gin and one percent something brown. Or maybe it was Scotch. No, then it would be called a Scotch. Her glance flitted to his face and she noticed he was watching her watch him, his smile curious. "What?" he asked.

She couldn't help herself and indicated his glass. "What's that, gin with a shot of cola?"

He made a disgusted face. "Hell, no."

She frowned, thinking. "Tequila and—and a touch of coffee?"

Laughter rumbled in his chest. "Right. I like to get drunk and sober up at the same time."

He was teasing her and that rankled. Now she *had* to know what a "Big Boy" was. "Well, what do you call it, then?"

He held up the glass for her to inspect. "I don't know what you cultivated city folks call it, but out here in the sticks we rednecks call it tea."

"Tea?" Her gut clenched. "You're drinking plain iced tea?"

"I'm the designated driver, sugar." He set down the glass. "Why?"

She experienced a shiver of distress. "It's not something called a—a Big Boy?"

He leaned forward as though he hadn't heard right. "A what?"

"Big Boy!" she shouted. "The waitress said that."

His lips quirked and he looked like he was fighting a grin. "Oh."

She knew he was laughing at her and she knew her cheeks were blazing. She was afraid she also knew that his "oh" confirmed why the waitress had used the term. Unfortunately, it didn't have a thing to do with what he drank. "What do you mean by 'oh'?" she cried, unable to fathom what screwball part of her psyche needed the answer to that question.

Garth ran a hand over his mouth. "I think it's time we danced." Standing, he neatly unstraddled his chair and took her hand. "This is a good tune for two-stepping."

She was so mortified by her Big Boy faux pas, the idea of being in his arms—brushing up against Mr. Big Boy—made her crazy. Needing a few minutes to compose herself, she withdrew her fingers from his. "Just…not now. I—I think I'll go find the ladies' room. I'll be—"

"Garth, *baby!*" came a shriek from behind her.

His glance lifted to somewhere over Deedee's head. "Adele."

Before Deedee could leap to safety, the eager female knocked her sideways to get at Garth. A minute later, he and the willowy, redheaded linebacker were arm in arm, heading for the dance floor. "—Right back," Deedee muttered sarcastically. "Why don't you go dance while I'm gone?"

She watched him disappear into the crowd, another female's fingers already caressing the hair at his nape. It was ridiculously clear why Garth had no interest in settling down with one woman. Without even the crook of a finger, he could have any woman in sight—*present company excepted,* she prayed.

Picking her way through the milling ocean of boots and Stetsons, her feet crunching on popcorn and cigarette butts, she passed the bar. Hearing a low groan, she stopped and looked around.

"It's the gawd-awfulist burn, Milt."

The forty-something cowboy who had spoken was sitting on the end stool. He leaned toward his companion. "Lookie there. Now that's gonna blister, ain't it?"

The other cowboy bent over and inspected the groaning cowboy's neck. "Looks pretty bad, Joe. How'd you get that?"

"Was my damn old woman's idea. She had me dig up her petunias and move 'em to another spot. Forgot my hat."

Milt guffawed. "Petunia burn?" He slapped his buddy on the back. "Now there's a real man's burn."

Joe sucked down the rest of his longneck beer. "Shut up, you goat-faced ol' hog." He groaned again. "It hurts like I got me a neck full of buckshot."

Deedee edged over to the sunburned man. "Excuse me?"

He shifted unsteadily and looked at her. His eyes didn't focus well, and she realized he was drunk. But that didn't matter. He was hurting and she could fix it. "I know how to make your neck feel better."

The cowboy named Joe scowled at her, most likely to get her better in focus. His face was jowly, his bulbous nose almost wide enough to hide his squinty eyes. "Huh?" He sat back, tottering slightly. When his eyes had a little time to absorb her image through the beer-induced fog around his brain, he smiled. "Wha'd you say, girlie?"

She hailed the bartender. "Sir? Do you have any apple cider vinegar back there?"

The massive barman lumbered over and leaned an elbow on the scarred bar. He smiled at her. His long graying hair was tied in a ponytail and a loose wisp hid one eye. "Yes, little lady?"

"Apple cider vinegar?"

He screwed up his pockmarked face. "You want to drink it?"

She laughed. "No. This man has a sunburn and apple cider vinegar helps take the sting out."

The bartender looked at Joe, then back at Deedee. With a shrug of his burly shoulders, he fished around under the bar. "Used to have a waitress who brought salad makin's for her supper. Disgustin' stuff." He made a squinty face, exposing chipped front teeth. Deedee wondered how many fights this place hosted nightly. "Yeah, yeah. Here we go. Still got half a bottle." He handed it to her.

"Uh—thanks. Now a cloth?"

He held out his bar towel. She took it, finding a dry spot that didn't look dirty. Wadding it, she swabbed the terry cloth with vinegar. "Now," she said to Joe. "Lean forward."

He gave his companion, Milt, a look. "Sure, girlie."

He splayed his elbows on the bar, plopping his jowly chin in his hands. Deedee carefully began to dab the vinegar onto his scarlet neck. "How does that feel?"

He grunted, then swiveled his head her way. "Stinks, but it feels better." He smirked, his tobacco-stained teeth a blotchy sepia in the bar's dim light. She went on dabbing until she felt she'd covered the entire burn. "That should do it. Just remember apple cider vinegar if this happens again." She noticed the bartender had wandered off to serve some drinks at the far end of the bar, so she placed the bottle and the rag beside Joe.

He sat up and swiveled to face her. She noticed that his beer belly was so large his shirt buttons strained over the paunch, showing glimpses of fish-white skin. "You're a right helpful gal." He grasped her wrist. "What's your name, gal?"

She tugged on her arm, but couldn't get free. Unlike Garth, Joe's grip hurt. "Uh—Deedee. I really need to go now."

"Hold on there, Deedee-dee," he said, his words slurred. "Me and Milt want to get to know you better." He leered at her and she felt naked. Dirty. Though her baggy clothes barely let on that she had any female attributes at all, Joe's expression told her he was willing to make a thorough search.

She yanked. "Just a minute, sir. I tried to be helpful. But if you think I have anything else in mind, you're wrong."

Joe chortled and faced his friend. "She talks nice, don't she, Milt? I like educated gals."

Deedee grew alarmed. For the first time in her life, she was frightened by the look in a man's eyes. Her heart hammered and she didn't know what to do. She wasn't the type to make a scene, but she wasn't crazy about her odds if she didn't. Joe lifted the arm that had been resting on the bar. A sweaty hand went for her breasts.

"Why, you…" She lurched sideways, but couldn't remove herself from his grasp. Lashing out, she struck him across the face. "Let go of me!"

Joe's smile faded. The place where she slapped him grew beet red. "Why, you're a little spitfire, ain't you, gal?" His beady eyes glittered with back-alley lust. It wasn't pretty. She jerked, but couldn't remove herself from his hammy grip. "Say, gal, why don't you, me and Milt go have us a party?"

She tried to back up, but ran into a doughy wall that had to be Milt. He'd gotten off his stool and was blocking their little scuffle from the view of others sitting at the bar. She panicked when Joe slid off his own stool and began to haul her toward the door. Milt slung an arm about her shoulders, his body odor making her gag.

Her mind flew in all directions, trying to recall anything of the eight-hour self-defense course she'd taken at the YWCA. Okay, she could elbow Milt, at the same time stomp on Joe's instep. Then, in that instant of pain and surprise, she'd launch herself off Joe's foot, break free and run like mad. Did that sound even vaguely doable?

They were nearly to the door so she didn't have many options. Sucking in a fortifying breath, she silently commanded, *On the count of three. One, two—*

"Excuse me, gents."

Deedee heard Garth's voice. Her heart tumbled over with relief when he stepped in front of Joe and Milt. "This young lady happens to be my guest." He glanced at her. He was smiling, but there was something different about the expression. Something malevolent. And she could detect a lethal glint in his eyes. Though she was being held captive by two burly men, Garth stood a head taller than either of them.

Deedee cast a glance at Joe and then Milt. It appeared that even sloshed they were able to calculate that two middle-aged, intoxicated doughboys were no match for one tall, muscular man with blood in his eye.

She stared at Garth. He continued to smile as he took off his hat and ran a hand through his hair. The move held a tinge of impatience and seemed somehow aggressive. The danger signals he gave off were as subtle as his dancing was sexy, but they were unmistakable. She stiffened. She didn't want to be the cause of a fight, and she already knew Garth's preferences on the subject.

"Deedee, sugar, I think it's our dance." He held out a hand.

She yanked once more and this time Joe let go. "Well, hell, Garth. She didn't say nuttin' about being with you." He staggered a step away, evidently hoping Garth's attention span was so short that he wouldn't recall Joe's participation at all.

Taking Deedee's hand, Garth winked at Joe. "Now you know." He eyed Milt, who made strangled, grunting sounds, no doubt meant as an apology. His smelly arm lifted from her shoulders and she dashed to the safety of Garth's side.

Sweeping her into his protective embrace, he guided her away without a backward glance.

She was jelly-legged and her breathing came in frail gasps. Joe's reddened finger marks indented her skin and she rubbed her throbbing wrist.

"What did I tell you, sugar?" Garth asked, sounding irritated now that they were alone.

She looked at him. His jaw bunched. "About what?"

"About being Little Miss Helpful Hints in here?"

She swallowed, shaking her head. "You said something about beer stains—but that guy had a sunburn. I was just rubbing vinegar on his neck."

He pursed his lips. "So that's why you smell like pickling day."

She winced, rubbing her hands on her jeans. Garth smelled like a man who could smell good for a living and *she* smelled like vinegar.

He exhaled, clearly exasperated. "Sugar, let me give you one of Garth's helpful hints." When he removed his arm from around her shoulders she experienced an odd sense of loss. "Take it from a card-carrying member of the good-ol'-boys club. Never rub a redneck's neck unless you're prepared to rub a whole lot more of him." His hand went to the small of her back, coaxing her onto the dance floor. "Let's two-step."

Three tunes later, Deedee felt as if she really knew how to do the dance. Garth was a good teacher—patient, and showing a sense of humor when her jogging shoes came down hard on his feet. After only fifteen minutes, she felt comfortable with the steps. And darn if she didn't feel comfortable in his arms. Well, maybe not comfortable, exactly. Her heartbeat was too rapid for comfort. But whatever she felt, she liked it.

He'd begun the lesson holding her a foot away from him as he taught her the steps. Now he'd taken her hand and placed it on his chest, covering it with his own. And he'd pulled her so close that they were rubbing bellies. Even so, they were dancing. She was dancing! He led so well, she always knew which way they were turning, even at such close proximity.

When she did screw up—and stared embarrassedly at his face—he just winked and led her in a thrilling little spin. She was amazed at how well they fit together on the dance floor. Of course, she hadn't seen any of his other partners stumble helplessly to their knees. She sighed, gazing at his shirtfront.

"What's with the sigh?"

At his murmured question, she jerked her gaze up to meet his flashing grin. Recovering from her surprise that he'd even noticed, she shook her head. "Nothing."

"Come on."

She felt stupid for giving away her feelings, and she certainly didn't plan to tell him what she'd been thinking about. On the other hand, she might as well tell him something that had preyed on her mind all evening. "Look, Garth," she said. "You and I both know it wasn't your idea to bring me here. I'm interfering with your—your..." She didn't quite know how to broach the subject.

"Pollinating?"

She found the soft way he said the word both disturbing and exciting, and she couldn't respond. She just looked at him, eyes wide and mouth open. She was embarrassed that he hadn't bought her story the other day about "partying." He'd heard her say "pollinating" and he'd remembered it. Her cheeks ablaze, she said, "Well—if you want to put it that way—yes."

His chuckle tingled all through her. "You're the one who put it that way, sugar."

Unable to look him in the eye, she murmured, "Why don't you take me home? You've done everything Clara wanted you to."

"Do you want to go?" His warm breath teased her forehead.

*No, I don't want to go!* she wailed inwardly. *I want to stay here, relishing the feel of your hard body. Of your hand holding mine against your heart, feeling the strong, steady beat. I want to put my head against your shirt and bite off the buttons! I want to lick your chest and I want you to lick—* "Yes," she blurted breathlessly. "I do. I want to go." Pushing away from him, she averted her gaze. "Now, if you don't mind."

"Okay, sugar."

He took her elbow, guiding her among the dancers. Naturally, they couldn't simply leave. Garth was accosted several times on the way to the door by clinging females, brokenhearted that he was going. He merely grinned and said he'd see them soon. Several more times he tossed off the question, "Marry me, darlin'?" Deedee assumed this was pretty much the normal way he left the Broken Spur. She managed to keep a smile pasted on her face until they were in the truck, then she slumped against her door.

"Tired?"

With her eyes closed, she nodded, but it was a lie. She wasn't tired at all. She was angry at herself for finding Garth Gentry so damnably irresistible. She was no better than the fawning women inside the club. And what was worse, she *knew* he was totally wrong for her. First, he was a cowboy, and secondly, "forever" was the last thing he planned to offer any woman.

The truck engine roared to life and she was relieved that he didn't try to make conversation. She preferred to ride along pretending she was alone—on a bus. A convent bus, full of nuns.

When they arrived at the house, Garth hopped out as she opened her eyes. She turned to get her door, but he was there before she could open it. "You don't have to do this, Garth," she objected, as he gave her a hand down. "I know you want to get back."

"Back?" He cocked his head, looking puzzled.

She frowned. "Back to the Broken Spur. You're just dropping me off, aren't you?"

He took her arm and led her up the porch steps into a pool of light. "What made you think that?"

She spun to face him, feeling awful. "I didn't expect...I mean, I don't want to ruin your evening. Of course you're going back."

He leaned against the wall next to the door, scanning her with those stunning, earthy eyes. "I had a fine time."

Her stomach twisted into a knot of guilt. "No...no, I mean...well, you didn't get a chance to..."

"What?" He grinned, then surprised her by pushing her

glasses more firmly in place. As he did, his finger skimmed the bridge of her nose. The simple touch bordered on erotic, making her giddy.

She rubbed the spot, wishing she didn't register the contact so singularly. She cleared her throat, backing away defensively. "Uh…" What were they talking about? Oh, yes. Garth's pollinating. "What I meant was, with all those women at the Broken Spur you've slept with, I thought you'd want to pick one out and—"

"Hold on there." He watched her, surprise on his face. "What makes you think I've slept with those women?"

"Well, I—I just…" She took another step backward, mortified, wishing she'd never brought this up. "Haven't you?"

He leaned toward her. "Let me get this straight, sugar. You want me to tell you about my sex life?"

Doubting it with all her heart, she chewed the inside of her lower lip. "Put that way—I guess it's none of my business."

"That's a fact." His expression grew openly amused. "But I'll make you a deal."

She crossed her arms before her in a protective move. He was so close his breath warmed her cheek. She took another step away. "What…what kind of a deal?"

"You tell me yours, then I'll tell you mine." His eyebrows rose in a silent dare.

She stared at him in disbelief. When she found her voice, she muttered, "You've made your point." Clamping her hands on her hips, she challenged, "But you had a dozen women hanging all over you this evening. Are you suggesting they don't know you very, very well?"

"I'm suggesting you could be wrong about me." He drew a step closer and she took another step away—into the wall. "Could be I'm not the rutting bull you think I am."

"Liar."

With one finger, he made a little sign of the cross over his chest. "Cross my heart."

The very air around her seemed electrified. There was something lazy and seductive about his look. She flattened herself against the peeling siding. "Well, I *know* you slept with the waitress."

"Nope."

Deedee peered at him, dubious. "Big Boy?"

His lips twitched. "Truth is, I'm the victim of some ugly powder-room gossip."

She didn't know why—she had no right to—but she felt almost buoyant. For some idiotic reason, she almost believed him. Women loved to talk about men, and the best stories spread like wildfire. It was possible he hadn't slept with them all. Maybe only one or two, and the rest were just eager to get lucky. *You're a bigger fool than even you thought,* she scoffed inwardly. But right now that didn't matter. She found herself smiling and she shook her head at him. "Cowboy, I know men who'd pay top dollar to be the victim of gossip like that."

His grin was quick and erotic. "Know 'em well, sugar?"

Heat rushed up her cheeks. This conversation had turned into a flirtation and was fast moving toward a seduction. Hers! She must pull herself together, ignore any warm fuzzies she'd begun to harbor for this man, stiff arm him out of her dreams and her personal space. He was too close and she could see in his eyes that he planned to get closer.

Her determination became a rock inside her and she pushed away from the wall, struggling to appear nonchalant. "I'll bet if you go back to the bar right now and crook your finger, some willing female will fall at your feet. Go on. I insist." She scurried around him to the door, tapping it with a finger. "Just unlick this for me first."

"Un*lick* it?" he asked, chuckling.

She cursed herself and she cursed Freud for inventing his stupid slip.

She stared at the door, refusing to look into those sparkling eyes. "Unlock," she gritted. "I said *unlock.*"

"Sure you did, sugar."

After he turned the key, he pushed open the door for her. "What do you say to a good-night kiss?"

She craned her neck, stunned. "A what?"

His expression charmingly boyish, he dipped his head, placing their lips in dangerous proximity. "Just between friends?"

She grew light-headed. Her emotions ping-ponged violently between *take me now* and *shoot me dead.* She wanted those lips against hers more than anything, but they were the wrong lips. Allowing her sexual urges to run away with her now would cause pain in the long run. With a mental shake, she faced him squarely, bravely. "I—I don't think that would be a good idea."

A slight narrowing of his eyes was his only physical reaction to her rejection. His smile didn't dim. "To be honest, sugar, there was one woman there tonight I have an urge to sleep with."

She backed into the house, but no farther than one small step. She didn't want to hear this, but she couldn't get her legs to obey her command to run. "Really?" she squeaked. "That's good. Why don't you sleep with her, then?"

He studied her for a moment, his grin fading. "Because she won't even let me kiss her good-night."

# 7

GARTH RUBBED SADDLE SOAP into his saddle, unable to stop thinking about last night. "Let me know when you get tired of me being a gentleman, sugar," he'd said. Deedee had just stared at him, unblinking.

Even after he'd gone upstairs, she'd stood motionless for a long time. When she'd finally moved, she'd looked around, then ran both hands through her hair.

Garth had watched her from the shadows at the top of the stairs as she sank to the bottom step. "I'm tired of it now," she'd whimpered. "But don't you dare stop!"

He cursed himself at the memory. Last night hadn't turned out the way he'd planned, at all. At first he'd been irritated with his grandmother for foisting Deedee off on him. He'd planned to turn the evening into a search for just the right, willing bed partner. Damn, he needed a woman. He hadn't been lying to Deedee when he'd implied he wasn't the rutting bull she thought he was. It had been a long time since he'd been with anybody. Maybe he was too picky. Maybe he was sick.

He smiled tiredly. No, he wasn't sick. He was bored. Why did he have to get bored with everything? First it had been his wife, then cutting competitions and now—heaven spare him—all women?

He sat back on the stool, closing his eyes. No, that wasn't true. He'd discovered after thirty minutes at the bar that he wasn't going to find anyone there to his liking. Those women hanging all over him bored him, turned him off. But that wasn't the case with the woman he'd come with. Deedee didn't bore him.

With a curse he dipped his cloth into the saddle soap and went back to rubbing. What the heck was the matter with him? He'd been restless and discontented, even when the most willing females draped themselves over him, making it clear what they wanted. No matter whom he danced with, his gaze kept wandering to the bespectacled little character at his table as she munched popcorn, looking small and out of place.

He'd watched her when she'd spoken to Joe, and frowned in consternation as she'd nursed the old reprobate's neck. Shaking his head, Garth recalled when Joe and Milt had started to drag Deedee outside. The weirdest protective anger had come over him and he'd broken away from his dance partner without even a "beg pardon," to rush to Deedee's aid.

Then he'd taught her the two-step. At first she'd been obviously uncomfortable. She was hard on herself with every misstep and he could tell she wanted badly to do everything perfectly. It was as easy to spot as a bull in a chicken coop that she was insecure about a lot of things, desperately wanting to excel in whatever she tried. And, damnation, he didn't see why she felt that way. She was smart, pretty, hardworking and, well...nice. She had a great smile, and those eyes—big, honest and passionate—could swallow a man whole.

With the back of his hand, he pushed a lock of hair off his brow, his lips twitching wryly. She'd smelled like vinegar the whole time they'd danced, and on the porch after they got home. He kept telling himself that vinegar was not a sensual smell. But that hadn't stopped him from having the insane urge to pull her down on a bed of lettuce and pour olive oil all over her.

Inhaling the vague sweetness of the saddle soap, he ran a hand over the soft leather he'd been working. For an instant, in his mind, it became Deedee's thigh, warm and yielding beneath his callused fingers.

With a black curse, he tossed his cloth on the table and jammed the lid on the saddle soap can. She was driving him nuts with that don't-touch-me stand of hers. What in thunder would be so wrong with one night in his bed? He wasn't asking for a lifetime commitment. Just a few hours of her time.

It wasn't as though she'd be the loser in the deal, either. He didn't take the gift of a woman's body for granted. It went against his grain to let women walk away from his bed unsatisfied. He did his damnedest to please. So what was Deedee's problem? She didn't honestly believe she had to be married, or engaged, to a man before she...

He stood up, planting his hat low on his brow. Were there still women like that out there? And men, too? He supposed it was possible. After all, hadn't he been that way with Jenny? It seemed like another life, it had been so long ago. But he'd been loyal to her. A one-woman man. While he'd been away at competitions, other women had given him opportunities to cheat, but he'd always gone home to his own bed and his own wife. Until that day—his twenty-seventh birthday—when he'd walked in the door to find Jenny gone.

With his jaws clamped tight, he left the tack room and headed for the house. He'd hardly minded when Jenny left, more surprised by her leaving than broken up. That realization had taught him a hard lesson. He was missing a gene or a chromosome or something deep down and fundamental that people needed to stay together forever. The sad, simple truth was Garth Gentry got bored with everything, sooner or later. So it would be cruel to get too involved with any one woman.

He heard the sound of a door closing and looked up to see Deedee step out the back door, into the garden. He scanned her as she maneuvered among rows of plants to reach the tomatoes.

She wore pink shorts. Not too pink and not too short— librarian walking shorts. Even so, the sight of her slender, pale legs had an uncomfortable effect on him. Her button-front shirt was modest, even mannish. But the oversize garment didn't fool him—there was one hundred percent woman in there. He'd held her in his arms last night, and no man felt like that.

Shrugging thumbs in his belt loops, he squinted, angling his head to watch as she bent to reach inside a wire cage to snag the reddest, ripest tomato. "Dang nice backside," he mumbled, wondering if she had any idea he was watching her. Maybe she was presenting her upturned tush on purpose, to make him crazy.

He recalled her pitiful little plea on the stairs last night when she'd thought she was alone. No, she wasn't doing anything of the sort. She really didn't want him to stop playing the gentleman. She really didn't know he was watching her. He ran a hand along his jaw, hoping there was another thing she would never know—that the smell of vinegar had become a very unorthodox turn-on for him, and probably would be for a while.

She straightened, a bright red tomato in each hand. He knew the instant she caught sight of him, for she froze. *Okay, missy, if you want a gentleman, that's what I'll be.* With a finger to the brim of his hat, he nodded. "'Morning, Miss Emerson."

He watched her cheeks go as pink as her shorts. Her

smile was hesitant. "Hi, Garth." She dropped her gaze to pick her way through the rows of vegetables.

He waited by the door and opened it for her, allowing her to precede him inside. Her glance was sidelong. "Thanks."

"'Welcome." He sniffed. No vinegar today. But something else. Lemons? He wondered if she'd been using lemon furniture polish, but decided not to dwell on it or breathe too deeply. He didn't think being turned on by household cleanser, turpentine, shoe polish and whatever else she saw fit to use would make his life less complicated. She'd already turned talcum powder, rubbing alcohol and vinegar into aphrodisiacs. That was plenty.

He hung his hat on a peg beside the door. By the sound of her sandals, he knew she'd moved to the far end of the kitchen. Running water told him she was washing the tomatoes. A boiling pot on the stove caught his eye, so he decided to serve himself lunch. He was starving. After she moved away from the sink to slice the tomatoes, he washed his hands, then took a bowl from a cabinet. Back at the stove, he began to ladle out soup. It startled him when a slice of lemon and a sock fell into his bowl.

"What the..." He thumped the steaming dish on the countertop, sloshing liquid. A few drops hit him, but not enough to burn. "What in hell?" He turned to stare at Deedee.

She spun toward him, a paring knife in her hand. "What's wrong?" Her pretty eyes were wide, apprehensive.

"Wrong?" He sidestepped so that he no longer blocked her view of the soup bowl. The toe of the white sock lolled on the countertop. Grasping it between two fingers, he held it up. "I don't think it's quite done."

She looked at the limp, dripping stocking, then at his

stern face. A smile began to form on her lips, gradually turning into a full-fledged grin. "You thought *that* was your lunch?"

There was something about her standing there grinning at him that made his aggravation disappear like smoke in the wind. He shrugged, dropping the sock into the bowl. "Stupid of me." He shook his head. "Everybody knows socks are traditionally served for supper." He joined her in a grin. "So June 14 is National Eat-a-Sock Day?"

She giggled and laid aside her knife before walking over to him. He couldn't find a gentlemanly instinct in his body strong enough to move away. Even so, she managed to keep from touching him as she picked up the bowl and dumped its contents back into the pot. "For your information, smarty-pants, if you boil clean but dingy athletic socks with lemon they come out sparkling white." With a saucy toss of her head, she went back to the other side of the kitchen to finish slicing tomatoes.

He followed her, leaning against the counter. "You're scary, you know that?"

She piled the tomato slices on a platter containing everything needed to make sandwiches. Glancing at him, she said, "I wouldn't have thought a few wet socks would frighten a *big boy* like—" She broke off and bit her lip. "I mean…" Grabbing the platter, she averted her gaze. "Lunch is ready," she mumbled. "Clara and Perry are already at the table."

After she disappeared into the dining room, he slumped against the counter. Running a hand over his eyes, he fought a surge of frustration. Damnation, she was sexy when she was flustered. He wanted so badly to take her in his arms and sweep her up the stairs to his bed—to show her in a thousand lusty ways that there was nothing to be flustered about.

So what if some silly female had nicknamed him Big Boy. Didn't she understand that might not be such a terrible thing? Couldn't she sense, deep in her soul, that he would do everything in his power to give her pleasure?

If she would only let him.

THE LUNCH DISHES DONE and the elderly Gentry couple upstairs napping, Deedee returned to the dining room. This afternoon she planned to get her resumé written and sent out. An old manual typewriter Clara had dug out of a closet sat on the table. Deedee took a seat before it and rolled in a piece of typing paper.

After fifteen long minutes of staring at the blank sheet, she started to type. Unfortunately, she didn't have much of a business or educational history. Her only newspaper credits had gone quickly from writing obituaries to the helpful-hints column, with nothing in between. And after leaving the farm, her first job had been working behind the counter at a burger joint. She doubted that particular vocational experience would hold much weight in the publishing world. She sighed. Well, she wanted to work at a newspaper, so she might as well try newspapers first. "They can't put you in jail for trying," she muttered.

"Depends on what you try, sugar."

Garth's voice made her jump. She twisted in her chair, slapping a hand to her chest. "Are you on heart-attack duty this afternoon? Because if you are, you're doing a great job."

His grin was dazzling, showing a decided lack of repentance. Curling his fingers around the back of her chair, he read what she'd typed so far. "Your memoirs?"

His knuckles grazed her back, and she hunched forward. "I—I'm going to start looking for a job."

"Oh?" He nodded. "Good idea." Reaching around her,

he picked up a creased piece of stationery that had been lying beside the typewriter. As he bent near, his aroma invaded her senses. He smelled good, like leather and sunlight. She inhaled, rebuking herself for finding so much enjoyment in any mere smell. "What's this?" he asked.

Miffed at her reaction to his nearness, she snatched the page from his fingers, thumping it onto the table and irritably smoothing it. "Don't you have something to do in the barn?"

"I'm done." He hiked a thigh onto the table. Lounging there, he leaned toward her. "So, how's the job hunting going?"

She shrank away from his nearness, crossing her arms. "I'm just starting to type my resumé to send to newspapers, if you must know."

With one finger, he flicked the page she'd snatched from him. "And what was this, again?"

"Bernie sent me that. He has a computer, so he compiled the addresses of a bunch of Oklahoma papers."

Garth cocked his head, angling nearer still. "Bernie the countess?"

She scowled at him. "Don't make fun."

His grin was teasing, charming—irritating. "Wait a minute, sugar," he reminded her softly, "calling Bernie a countess was his idea, not mine."

She felt foolish for lashing out. Quite possibly the blame for her short temper could be placed in the way Garth lounged there. He'd propped his dratted, muscular thigh almost in her direct line of vision. Worse than that, the buttoned fly of his jeans was a bit too accessible and welcoming. When her glance made the mistake of wandering there, the jeans-clad bulge seemed to smirk. *Hi, sugar, I'm Mr. Big Boy.* An aberrant charge of arousal sizzled through her body, and she panicked. Gulping hard, she compelled herself to stare only at the typewriter keys. "Well—whatever—I really need to get this done."

The table creaked, signaling that he was getting up. She closed her eyes, weak with gratitude that he was taking her hint—however blatant—and going away.

A knock at the front door drew her glance.

"I'll get it." Against her better judgment, she watched him amble through the parlor. Cowboy poetry in motion.

When he opened the front door, Deedee saw a woman standing there. "Hi, Garth." The newcomer smiled and Deedee shifted in her chair to get a better look. She was tall, very, very blond and pretty—big surprise.

"Hi, darlin'," he drawled. "Want to come in?"

The woman didn't need her arm twisted. Long, practically bare legs swept her into the tiny entryway. "Thanks," she said with a breathy smile. "I just barely made it here."

"Really?" Garth took her arm and steered her into the parlor. They stepped around Old Dawg, sound asleep and negligently unperturbed that some strange female was sniffing around his master. Unfortunately, the dog was probably accustomed to that.

"I heard you were staying at your grandparents' for a while." The woman tossed her hair, fluffing it like a model preparing for a photo shoot. She topped off the coquettish performance by licking her lips. "Lucky for me you're here. See, my car's gas gauge was flashing empty, but I managed to make it almost all the way down the drive."

Garth's expression grew sympathetic, but there was the glitter of amusement in his gaze. "That was lucky."

She nodded, smoothing her bright, gauzy summer frock. Deedee typed one letter, then found herself eyeing the young woman again. She wasn't wearing a bra, and Deedee had serious concerns about a lack of panties, too.

"Isn't there a gas station on down the road about a hundred yards?" Garth asked.

The woman flushed. "Uh, well, I wasn't sure I could make it." She toyed with a button on his shirt. "Since I made it here, I was wondering if you'd help fill me up?"

Except for the laughter in his eyes, he appeared to buy her flimsy story. "Be my pleasure, darlin'." Taking her arm, he led her to the door.

"You're the sweetest man, Garth," she cooed.

The door closed and Deedee couldn't do anything but gawk. "I was wondering if you'd help fill me up!" How transparent could the little conniver be? And could Garth have been *more* willing to swallow that baloney? Hardly.

The sound of his truck's engine igniting caught her attention, and she grimly faced the typewriter. What difference did it make to her if Garth was going off to fill her up? She choked at the indecent image the words conjured, shoving it from her brain. She needed to get her resumés written and mailed out. Determined, she began to pound the stiff old keys.

After a few minutes of concentrated typing, she found her attention snagged by the last line she'd written. To her horror, it said, "and for the past three years I wrote a newspaper column called Winnie's Helpful Sex in Garth's pickup."

Moaning, she lowered her forehead to the table. This was *not* going well.

BACK FROM THE GAS STATION, Garth pulled his truck to a stop beside the blonde's middle-aged sedan. "Here we are, darlin'. While I put gas in the tank, why don't you go sit on the porch swing?"

She smiled, but he saw disappointment in her honey brown eyes. Aggravated with himself, he jumped out of the truck and headed for her car. He wasn't being much of a gentleman. He hadn't introduced this little twinkie to Dee-dee, and he wasn't opening her door for her. First, he didn't remember her name and second, he wasn't interested in exploring that long, lean body she seemed so bent on throwing his way. The sooner he got her gassed up and gone, the better.

As he jerked off the gas cap, he heard the other truck door slam. The blonde was mad, but that was her problem. He had problems of his own. He stuck the gas can's spout into the tank and poured. Fumes stung his nostrils as he berated himself. *Thunderation, Garth, with the energy you wasted appeasing that blonde, you could have had great sex and been done with it. Bang! The end of your horny daydreams about Miss Emerson. But, no! You'd rather make yourself miserable, fantasizing about Deedee with her soft, round hips and don't-touch-me-cowboy glare, than get some much needed relief from this willing cutie-pie.*

He heard a door open and looked up to see Dawg tramp outside, followed by Deedee. She peeked toward Garth, but quickly broke eye contact. "Okay, Dawg," she called. "Do your business. It's hot out here."

The dog raced down the steps and disappeared around the side of the house. Deedee slowly followed. When Garth finished pouring the gas, he screwed the cap on, his gaze snagging Deedee's again. She smiled without much enthusiasm, then hustled to the corner of the house. But she didn't disappear. She stayed there, presenting her back to him.

As he stepped away from the car, he bumped into the blonde. "Oh—sorry, I didn't see you." He'd completely forgotten about her.

He thrust out an arm to steady her. Apparently she took it as an invitation, for she coiled her arms about his neck.

"This was wonderful of you," she said, her voice ripe with sexy promises. "You know what? I'm going right home to bake you a big chocolate cake."

He laughed, trying to mean it. "My favorite. Marry me, darlin'?"

She giggled. Stretching up to meet his lips, she kissed him hard and frantically, rubbing her body provocatively against his. Being a healthy heterosexual male, he squeezed his eyes shut, resisting acting on involuntary responses he couldn't help. She was making it clear that he could throw her down in the grass right now and take care of his problem. But damn him, he didn't want whoever she was. He wanted Deedee Emerson.

It took all of his self-control to peel her off and get her into her car.

"You take care, now," she called out her window as she drove off.

Idling against his pickup fender, he waved her away. Once she was out of sight, he eyed heaven, exhaling tiredly. At that moment, he heard familiar scampering sounds. Glancing down, he saw his scruffy mutt in the process of leaping up to plant his paws on Garth's chest.

"Oof! Dawg!" He brushed the forepaws away. "Get down, you ol' dustmop." Squatting, he gave Old Dawg an affectionate rubbing as a rough tongue left wet streaks along his neck. "Okay, we'll play stick." When he stood, he was surprised to see Deedee sitting on the bottom step of the porch. "Hi," he said, pleased that she hadn't gone inside.

She stood. "If you're going to play with him, I'll go finish my resumé."

He nodded. "Sure. Thanks for letting him out."

She shrugged. "No problem." She turned away, then

stopped. After a few seconds, she faced him again, her expression troubled. "Garth?"

He walked onto the grass and scooped up a stick. Showing it to his dog, he gave it a good, long toss. The mutt was after it like a coyote going for a campground. Facing her, Garth cocked his head, wondering what was bothering her. "Yes?"

"Aren't you afraid one of these days one of your women will sue you for breach of promise?"

Her subject choice surprised him and he frowned, confused. "What?" He took a step toward her and was annoyed when she moved backward, up one step.

She waved in the direction the blonde had gone. "Like that—that *blondie*. You just proposed to her, you know. And at the Broken Spur last night you asked no less than half-a-dozen women to marry you. And those are just the ones I heard." Deedee pushed her glasses into place, looking a little put out. "Don't you think, someday, one of them will take you seriously?"

He reached the bottom step and was butted in the rear by his dog. "Hey, no goosing." He turned, took the stick and gave it another hard throw before glancing at her again. "I bet you think *blondie* can cook, too." He lifted a skeptical brow.

Her face turned a cute shade of crimson and he watched her swallow several times. "Okay, so maybe I'm naive...." Her words died away and she cleared the hoarseness from her voice. "I guess there's safety in numbers," she mumbled, almost to herself. "If you're hauled into court you can produce the five hundred waitresses, store clerks, dental hygienists and the occasional female who shows up in your driveway out of gas, and prove you've proposed to them all. The case would get thrown out of court."

"Something like that." He lifted a boot to the first step.

She moved backward again, but didn't quite make the step, falling hard on her bottom. "Ouch!" She winced, leaning sideways to rub her bruised posterior. Frowning at him, she shrugged. "Well, if proposing to every woman you meet works for you, I guess it's none of my business."

"That's true." He took the remaining stairs two at a time and grasped her elbow. "We have some liniment. I could rub some on your hip."

She was halfway to a standing position when he made the offer. She shot a look at his face and her eyes went wide. "I beg your pardon?" Disdain rang in her tone.

He pulled her to her feet, aiming her toward the front door. "You heard me, sugar."

She jerked from his grasp. "You are *amazing*. Is it your usual habit to jump off one woman right onto the next?"

He opened the door for her, but when his glance met hers, he wasn't smiling. "No, Miss Emerson, it isn't."

For a fleeting moment their gazes clashed. It frustrated him to see both fear and longing in her eyes. An instant later, the door slammed in his face. With a curse on his lips, he turned and was met with the comical sight of his dog bounding up the steps, the stick lolling between his lips like a crooked cigar. Garth grinned, but experienced little true enjoyment. Sinking down to sit on the porch, he sagged against the door.

"Damn woman." He absently stroked his dog. "She treats me like rusty barbed wire." He took the sopping stick from his pet's mouth and listlessly tossed it off the porch. It didn't fall much farther than the steps, but Dawg didn't seem to mind. He was after it like a shot.

Running both hands through his hair, Garth made a promise to himself. He'd done everything her way long enough. Things were going to go *his* way, for a change. If it went on like this much longer, he'd be permanently disabled.

By thunder, he would prove to her what she insisted on denying—that they could make damn fine music together. And what they shared would be good for both of them.

He would coax her into his bed, make wild love to her and get her out of his system once and for all—the quirky little glasses-wearing, helpful-hints-peddling, vinegary, big-eyed botheration.

TUESDAY NIGHT, Deedee sat alone in the Gentrys' parlor. Clara and Perry had gone into Tulsa to play Bingo, and Garth had gone back to his place on Keystone Lake to take care of some things. Dawg was curled up beside Perry's easy chair. When he perked up his ears, Deedee knew Garth was back even before she heard his truck.

She would have preferred that he not come back right now, but it couldn't be helped. When the front door opened she squinted in that direction to see him stride in. He glanced her way and stilled with his Stetson halfway to the coatrack. After a momentary hesitation, he leaned farther into the parlor to frown at her. "What are you doing?"

She continued to suck on her cigar, watching the ash glow, then blew out foul-tasting smoke. Removing the disgusting thing from her mouth, she made a face. "I—I'm smoking a cigar." She coughed, then stuck it between her lips to suck again.

Garth dropped his hat on its hook and rounded the corner to stand in front of her. Waving away the cloud of smoke, he eyed her with a mixture of confusion and amusement. "Like I always say, there's nothing like a good cigar to bring up a meal."

He might have a point. Her stomach roiled. She pulled the half-smoked cigar out of her mouth and tried to smile, but she didn't feel well enough to keep her mouth open very long. With a shaky hand, she flicked ashes into a mayonnaise jar lid.

"You're green." He bent down, taking the flaming brown monster from her fingers.

"No," she cried weakly, but opted not to make a grab for it, since she didn't care to hurl her dinner all over the parlor. "I need that."

"I hear those are the last words junkies say before they die." He lifted the cigar to eye it. "Where did you get this thing? Grandpa gave up smoking ten years ago."

"Oh…" She swallowed, trying to keep her dinner down. "That's probably why it tastes like dirt."

Garth crushed it out in the mayonnaise lid. "What brought on this need to smoke?"

Sinking back on the sofa, she managed to lift one arm, though it felt as heavy as lead. "For that."

"The *National Geographic?*" he asked. "They having some kind of weird contest?"

She shook her head and pushed herself up so she could indicate the water ring on the coffee table. It was right beside the *National Geographic* Perry had been reading before he and Clara left for the bingo parlor. "Ashes are good for removing white water rings."

Garth squatted, running his hand over the ring, then lifted his gaze to her face. His grin was slow and sexy. "I don't know many woman who would risk their health for a coffee table."

She closed her eyes and groaned. That might have been funnier if her stomach hadn't been playing kick ball with her kidneys.

"Did you ever think about the fireplace?" She heard the sound of his boots as he crossed the room. When she peered at him, he was kneeling before the hearth. He reached behind the wire mesh screen and drew out an ashy fingertip. "Wouldn't these have worked?"

She already felt awful and now she felt awful and stupid. With a moan, she let her head loll away from him. "Oh fine. I'm going to die for nothing."

"Come on." After a second, she felt a hand on her wrist. "You need fresh air."

She didn't want to move, but he was insisting her wrist go with him, so she decided she'd better tag along. She felt bad enough without losing a body part, too. Once outside, he led her to the porch rail and surprised her by hoisting her up to sit on it. Clinging to the vertical support, she slumped against it. With her eyes closed, she prayed to die.

"Breathe," he said. "It'll help."

She obeyed with a vengeance, breathing so deeply she was afraid she was going to black out.

"Feeling better?"

She thought maybe she did, and nodded, though she didn't want to chance opening her eyes. She knew he was very near; she could detect his scent. Luckily, it didn't add to her nausea.

His low chuckle drew her gaze and she was stunned by the beauty of his smile. "Where did you find that damn cigar?"

Shy and embarrassed, she shook her head. "Magnolia found it. She was dragging it to the nest she made under my dresser." She giggled, startled to discover she felt almost normal. "I guess it's lucky I caught her, because she'd wadded up those hundred-dollar bills and stuffed them in there, too."

"I could tell when I met Magnolia she was a saver," he murmured, curling an arm around the porch support. When his fingers grazed Deedee's, she experienced a pleasant jolt, feeling no urge to move away.

She met his gaze again and her heart lurched madly. His head had dipped nearer, and his lips were now extremely close to hers. She cleared her throat, trying to appear unaffected, but she didn't believe she was fooling anybody—especially not Garth. She sensed he could tell she was dying to be kissed.

His lips lifted in a crooked half grin, and as though he read her thoughts, he slipped her glasses off. "I'm going to kiss you now," he murmured.

She couldn't summon words, but managed a small nod and a welcoming smile.

His mouth covered hers, his kiss leisurely, thoughtful, like a gift rather than a sneak attack. She swayed slightly and his arm came around her, steadying, cuddling. Lifting his mouth from hers, he gazed into her eyes. The teasing was gone and he seemed almost shocked by something.

She was dizzy, seeing double, so she couldn't be sure what she saw in his gaze. But she knew what she felt, and it didn't have anything to do with her recent hyperventilating. Garth knew how to kiss a woman. No question about that.

He leaned down and she sensed her lips were his intended target. Though she understood all the reasons why she should end this craziness now, she couldn't do a thing but angle her head up to meet his kiss. Her worst fears had been realized. Garth had kissed her and she was lost, her body humming with need and expectation.

This time when their lips met, she kissed him back with all the hunger that had been building inside her since the moment they'd met. His lips were the texture of fine velvet, thrilling her to her core. She hugged his wide, strong back, her fingers caressing, clutching.

His kiss was sweet, punishingly so, as he massaged provocatively, tenderly, yet with a sensuous insistence she couldn't deny. With lush, subtle messages his lips, his teeth, coaxed her to open her mouth, allowing him hungry access. While he explored, she tasted him, loving the wild new sensations he engendered, and her fervor became a fiery longing.

Their tongues danced together in silent harmony and he groaned against her mouth. Deedee reveled in the sexy, throaty sound, clinging even more desperately to him.

Suddenly, she was in his arms and he was carrying her inside. "Here's one of Garth's helpful hints," he said in a husky growl, nipping at her earlobe. "Don't smoke big, black cigars before sex." He thrust his tongue in her ear and she quivered with delight.

"But—but…" Her voice was weak and thready, the last vestiges of her sanity hanging on for dear life. "I'm not going to—to have sex."

His laughter rumbled through her body as he carried her up the stairs. "Wanna bet, sugar?"

# 8

SHE BECAME AWARE of his lips moving against her temple and his warm breath gentle on her cheek. He said something. She opened her eyes, but slowly, feeling sweetly drugged. "Hmm?"

His grin flashed. "I asked do you want the lights on or off?"

She flinched. "Off." The idea of the body she knew and didn't wholly love being displayed under a hundred-watt bulb was not an appetizing thought.

His chuckle was deep and pleasant against her breasts. "Spoilsport." He whisked her to his bed, and she was surprised when he sat her down rather than stretching her out on her back. When her feet touched the floorboards, she gazed at him, confused. He knelt before her, smoothing back her hair. His gaze roamed over her face, along her throat to the top button of her shirt. "I want to do this myself." She tingled at the husky sound of his voice and a rush of renewed longing warmed her blood. His gaze lifted to meet hers, his luscious eyes midnight black and glittering in the dim light.

She smiled timidly, grateful that the light from the barn gave off little illumination this far away. Her cheeks had to be scarlet.

He drew near, kissing the hollow at her throat, and she closed her eyes, allowing her whole being to concentrate on his mouth and tongue. Lifting her chin, she granted him freer access. Growing weak at his sensual touch, she leaned back, supporting herself with her hands as he unfastened that top button. His lips and teeth and tongue delighted her flesh as he spread the fabric, moving downward to dispose of the next small barrier, then the next.

She lolled her head back as he progressed, tasting, tempting, slowly, very slowly. She began to shudder, so overcome her limbs were trembling. When he pushed her shirt off her shoulders, the soft cotton fell on top of her fingers. The thought entered her mind to help him remove it by lifting her hands, but when his mouth closed over her breast, through the thin fabric of her bra, she gasped in awe, forgetting everything else.

Her heartbeat doubled and she arched into him. His arms came around her, holding her close, galvanizing her with the hot, wet suckling. She felt consumed, beautifully so. She was shocked by her eager response, and wrenched herself from her shirtsleeves to press him closer. She'd never felt such heady sexual heat. His tongue felt right, stroking the damp fabric, teasing, his teeth sampling. She moaned and writhed, loving the wild, hedonistic pull as he mouthed her breast, taking her in, gorging himself, yet not really touching her.

Blood pounded in her brain as currents of desire pulsed through her. Insane for him, needing body-to-body contact, she whimpered, grasping the strap of her bra and yanking it down so that his lips, his mouth, would touch her flesh.

When she did, he paused and their eyes met. He didn't smile and neither did she. Her breathing was hard, her throat dry. "Don't tease me, Garth," she cried. He blinked, scanning her face. And even though she wasn't wearing her glasses, she sensed his confusion. "You don't need to prime the pump," she said. "I'm primed. Make love to me."

"I thought that's what I was doing," he whispered.

She smiled wanly, the perplexity in his voice appealing. He seemed suddenly unsure, vulnerable, making him even more desirable. "Take off your clothes," she coaxed, grasping his shirt above the first button and yanking. When buttons began popping off, clattering on the wood floor, he glanced down at his ravaged shirt in disbelief, then up at her. His lips curved in a wry grin. "Who are you, sugar?"

She stood up, unhooking her bra and tossing it aside. With a supporting hand on his shoulder, she said, "Take off my jeans." She listened to herself with a vague sense of unreality. She didn't know herself. Something had broken inside her—or broken open, was more like it. The experience was eerie but exhilarating. When he shifted, possibly to stand, she held him down. "From there."

He looked up, this time grinning broadly. "Okay. You let me know if I do anything wrong."

She smiled this time, really smiled, amazed at herself. "Who are you?" was a legitimate question. She was no longer sure herself.

As his fingers snaked her zipper down, she inhaled a quick, sharp breath of appreciation. Then warm, callused hands at her waistband pressed her jeans down, down until they were around her ankles. With her hand still on his shoulder, she stepped out of them, leaving her sandals behind as she did.

Their eyes met, but no words were necessary. He knew what she wanted, and she could tell that he was fine with it. Her panties skimmed along her thighs, over her knees, then were discarded with the jeans.

"Sugar, I'd suggest you sit."

"Make me," she taunted, aghast at whoever this vixen was who had invaded her body and— "Oh..." she gasped, as Garth used his hand wickedly, making her knees buckle.

When she landed on the bed, she couldn't even sit upright and sagged backward. "Oh, Garth…"

His throaty laugh was deliciously sinful as his hands slipped beneath her knees, drawing them up and out. "Don't bother me, sugar," he whispered, his lips caressing her most intimate, feminine portal. "I'm busy."

She arched, moaning in delight as his mouth, his teeth, his tongue, gave her pleasure she'd never imagined. Breathless, she grasped at the bed covering, seeing star bursts behind her eyelids as he ministered to her, driving her to higher and higher plateaus—needing no guidance, no orders, no pleas. He seemed to understand her cries and sighs, fulfilling her needs though she had no words or voice to explain them.

Molten ribbons of sensation burned a path down her stomach to her legs. She couldn't breathe and gasped for air, fearing she would die. She reached for him, burying her hands in his hair. She wanted to pull him away, to stop the exquisite torture before it killed her. "Garth!" she cried, breathless, weak. "Please…"

He didn't lift his head, refused to obey. She tossed her head from side to side; tears filled her eyes. "Oh—*oh*…"

Clever, steady thrusts of his tongue sent her reeling, her high-pitched whimpers in rhythm with his deep kisses. For a dizzying instant she hovered between heaven and hell.

All at once, the earth exploded around her and she whirled and tumbled off into glorious oblivion. Twisting her fingers in his hair, she pulled, arched upward, shrieking out her exultation from the depths of her being.

Finally, leaving behind no regrets, she died a dazzling, fiery death.

"Are you awake?" he murmured near her ear.

She opened her eyes, turning to look at his marvelous face. She smiled shyly, wondering at herself. "I think I'm dead,'' she said, her voice hoarse, thready. Without her glasses he was hazy, haloed in the far-off, golden light from the barn. He seemed almost otherworldly, too marvelous to be human. ''Are you an angel?'' she asked, only half teasing.

His teeth flashed in a crooked grin. ''Not likely.''

His soft, sexy remark sent a tingle of appreciation skittering along her spine. Kissing the tip of his nose, she murmured, ''Well, whatever you are, you do good—deeds.''

He winked. ''Just following orders, ma'am.''

She remembered how uncharacteristically she'd acted, and chewed on her lower lip. ''I can't believe I did that.''

He reached up and smoothed a curl off her forehead. She was startled to realize it was damp. ''I was a little surprised myself,'' he said, his low laugh welcome and reassuring.

''I'm not usually bossy in bed....'' She caught herself. It wasn't as though she'd been in that many beds. Just Ty's, and things had gone rather—well, normally. Boy on top. Pleasant sensations. Over. ''I—I mean...'' She shrugged a shoulder, which Garth promptly kissed.

''You can boss me anytime in bed, sugar.'' He sat up. ''So, what's next?''

She looked up at him. Here she was naked, damp and satisfied, while he lounged beside her, dressed, except for a few badly abused buttons, spread Lord knew where. That realization was disconcerting, and she felt a rush of embarrassment.

''Something wrong?'' he asked, his voice low, almost wary.

Her unease must have shown in her face. She ran a hand through her hair, looking at him sheepishly. ''I just realized I'm the only one naked here.''

He grinned. ''I noticed that some time ago, sugar. You need to keep up.'' Pressing a curl behind her ear, he caressed her earlobe, sending shivers of pleasure through her. "Give me an order, boss lady," he whispered. "You're in charge."

His easygoing charm and his gentle touch made her feel less embarrassed. She was in charge, huh? That sounded promising. Bolstered by his encouraging smile and his nuzzling fingers, she propped herself up on an elbow, pretending to look thoughtful. "I think..." She sat up. "No." She shook her head. "I think I'm done," she teased, hopping off the bed. She thrilled when a strong arm came around her waist, pulling her back.

Garth's sexy growl was a turn-on all by itself. "That's not funny, sugar."

She giggled, snuggling in his arms. "I thought it was."

When his hand dipped to tease between her legs, all her playfulness melted away, and she went limp against him. "Oh...that's not fair."

"What?" Amusement tinged his voice. His hand began to work magic as his lips burned hot messages into her shoulder and neck. "I ask again," he murmured, his lips brushing her temple. "What do you want to do now?"

She pressed her face to his chest, kissing him. When his hands cupped her bottom, she groaned with pleasurable anticipation. "You have on too many clothes, Garth."

His laugh deep and sexy, he kissed the top of her head. "That's my girl."

She fumbled with his belt buckle, but couldn't get it undone. "Oh..." she groused. "What has your belt got against me?"

He brought his hands to her waist and shifted her over onto the bed. "Damn belt goes in the trash tomorrow." She lay on her side as he slid to the edge of the bed and pulled off his boots and socks. He stood, shrugging out of his shirt. The belt unfastened easily for him, and very soon he discarded the rest of his clothes to rejoin her on the bed. "Is this better?"

She reached out, running her hand over his chest, enjoying the masculine texture of muscle and springy hair.

"If you get to touch, then I get to touch," he said with a playful grin.

She drew nearer until her breasts brushed his chest. "What do you want to touch?" She trailed a finger up to outline his lips. "I'm very strict about touching. I don't let just anybody touch just anything."

He put an arm around her, pressing her hips into intimate contact with his groin. "You let me know when I go out of bounds, sugar," he said, his voice rough with desire.

She closed her eyes, relishing his arousal. When he began to kiss her face, she turned her mouth to meet his and once again accepted the gift of his lips, hot and hungry, against hers.

She hugged him hard, her breasts gloriously crushed against his powerful chest as their kisses deepened and their smoldering passions ignited into flame.

Garth's touch was provocative and she burned under his knowing fingertips. She'd never dreamed hands could be so gentle, so loving and sensitive to a woman's needs. Her stomach, her thighs, her throat, her back—no part of her went unexplored. He worshipped her in lusty, wanton ways, and she gloried in wave after wave of bold, new experiences.

At last he slipped on protection and positioned his body over hers. She opened herself to him, her longing to know him fully, burgeoning to lethal levels.

"*Now*, Garth," she pleaded. "Love me *now*."

Poised above her, he met her gaze. Those earthy eyes glowed with purpose and she smiled at him, sensing he would not disappoint her.

Garth didn't say anything, didn't return her smile. He merely dipped his head to kiss her. As he did, he thrust his pelvis forward, and her lips opened in an awed, whispery, "Oh."

Lifting his head, he drew himself up, then thrust again, deeper. This time a cry of delight escaped her lips. She stared up at him, her eyes wide, unblinking. When he thrust again, she arched to meet him. Licking her lips, she felt tears well in her eyes. His next thrust was deep, wicked, and she moaned with intense pleasure.

The tempo of his lovemaking increased as he continued to plunge, again and again, into her softness. With each blinding surge she thrilled, welcoming the invasion with all her foolish heart. She exalted in his male strength and the potent beauty of his passion. She was astonished by the sense of completeness she felt, connected to him in this most intimate way.

She met the full strength of his passion with equal passion of her own, reveling in the sweet agony of his hard, surging body. Their gratification climbed and climbed, their bodies heaving in a lush, primeval rhythm. Her breathing came in surrendering moans as he drove her deliciously up—up—over the edge. Fire bolts of ecstasy raced through her, shattering her into a million white-hot shards of absolute fulfillment.

As her body shuddered with her orgasm, she felt him jerk inside her, finding his own release.

She didn't know how long she lay beneath him, wrapped in the afterglow of their lovemaking. His slow, tender kisses along her temple brought her eyes open, and she shifted to meet his lips with her own. "I knew we'd be good together, Dee," he whispered huskily.

She relished the feel of his lips against hers, whispering sweet nothings. And his use of "Dee" instead of the more generic "sugar" made her feel oddly special—as though he was talking to her, not just his latest conquest. She curled her arms about his neck, surprised at how weak she was. She kissed him hard, almost desperately, for she realized something in her heart—something she didn't want to think about, because it made her sad.

Even now, still glowing with her climax, lying there all toasty and protected, covered by Garth's glorious body, she knew.

This would never happen again.

THE NEXT TWO DAYS dragged by as though they were weighted with stones. Deedee couldn't seem to turn around without Garth standing there, grinning at her. It almost seemed as though he didn't believe their one-night sexual spree was over—that he thought she wanted him again. What nerve! What gall! What distressing insight!

She tried to think of Garth as a lustful, egotistical womanizer, but she couldn't make it work. He really wasn't. He couldn't help it if he was sexy and gorgeous, or that women threw themselves at him. And as for the nickname...

She sucked in a shuddery breath. He certainly came by it honestly.

She gulped down another big breath, trying to calm her erratic heartbeat as the hot memories flooded back. Shaking her head, she forced her mind to what she was doing and sprinkled more baking soda over Garth's dog. "Sit still, silly." She rubbed the stuff into his fur. "Just another few minutes and I'll brush you."

"Lucky dog."

Deedee was squatting on the grass beside the front porch when she heard Garth's soft-spoken compliment. Jerking around, she lost her balance and fell to her backside. "You scared me,'' she charged, trying to keep her voice free of lovelorn overtones.

He drew near and knelt beside her, his scent carried to her by a fiendish breeze. His eyes glinted with things she didn't want to dwell on. Withdrawing her gaze, she turned to Dawg and rubbed.

"What are you doing, Dee?" Garth asked, using the same abbreviation for her name he'd used ever since their night together.

Her heart refused to settle into its regular beat and kept on pounding, pounding, pounding, in a savage reminder of—of his thrilling—

"Dee? Did you hear me?"

"Yes." She closed her eyes, drew on her dwindling reservoir of strength, then faced him. "I'm dry-cleaning Dawg." She eyed Garth levelly, trying to appear at ease, which was a mammoth effort. "He'll be deodorized as well as clean."

Garth's eyes shone beautifully as he smiled, and she inhaled sharply at the sight. "Just don't kill my dog, sugar," he teased.

That remark had become a joke between them, but Deedee didn't feel like laughing—not even smiling.

His grin faded and he touched her hand. She yanked it away as though she'd been electrocuted, which wasn't far from the way she felt.

"Look, Dee, I don't know what I've done wrong, but I'm sorry."

A lump rose in her throat. "Don't be silly," she rasped. "You haven't done a thing."

"Then…" he smoothed a strand of hair away from her eyes "…why the freezer act? I thought you and I had something pretty wonderful going."

Her stomach clenched and she tore her eyes away, casting around for the dog brush. "What we had—" Her voice broke and she swallowed around the painful lump. "What we had was one night, Garth," she said sternly. "I'd think that would be your limit, anyway."

She felt the brush being removed from her hand. Turning, she watched as he took up the grooming, but his eyes remained on her. Some shadowy emotion glittered in their depths. "Why do you say that?" he asked. "Why would I want that?"

She abruptly stood, finding his nearness difficult to bear. "If you're going to brush your dog, I ought to get back inside."

When she turned to go, he grasped her wrist. "Why does it have to be over? I thought you enjoyed yourself, too."

Tears welled and she blinked them back, grateful that she was facing away from him. "I'm not as into enjoying myself as you are." She jerked on his hold, but he didn't release her.

"I like you, Dee," he whispered, standing up. He slipped an arm around her, tugging her against him, into his hardness, and her breath caught. His breathing ruffled her hair, warm and stimulating. "I don't want it to end this way."

She couldn't stand the feel of him. No, that was a lie. She loved the feel of him. But she couldn't stand the fact that he was tempting her to prolong their affair—to make a hopeless situation worse than it already was. Did he think she had forgotten the love they made so beautifully together? Did he think she hadn't been affected, that she would *ever* be able to forget him? Did he really believe that a few more times would make their ultimate parting easier?

She slapped his arm away and whirled on him, backing a safe distance from his exciting body. "You don't want it to end this way?'' she jeered. ''Tell me, Garth, what way *do* you want it to end?''

He stared, his brows dipping. ''What are you talking about?''

She choked on a sad laugh. ''Oh, good, act confused. That probably works for you a lot.''

He reached for her, but she staggered away. ''I know your philosophy, Garth,'' she retorted. ''You don't get involved.''

He stilled, stared, but didn't speak.

She nodded, as though acknowledging his unspoken affirmation. ''Don't worry, your philosophy is fine with me. I don't want to get involved with you, either.'' Shoving her glasses into place, she hissed, ''And since our philosophies match so perfectly, I think we've been as involved as we need to be. *Forget* the other night.''

His dark eyes flashed. ''But why deny ourselves something so good?''

Her heart hammered foolishly with the need to run into his arms, to feel the heat of his body again, to experience the exhilaration of his kisses. But she already teetered dangerously near her emotional breaking point. Something had to make him stop this—to leave her alone before she weakened, allowing him to coax her into a prolonged affair that would permanently damage her heart. She had to find a weapon against him, but all she had was words.

Words! Couldn't they be as deadly as bullets? Of course! She had her weapon, after all. Gathering her courage, she eyed him with as much derision as she could muster, then lost her courage. Her glance flitted distractedly to his truck, the dog, the sky. ''Garth,'' she began, her voice raw and low. ''It wasn't that good for me.''

Her lie tasted like ashes in her mouth, but she couldn't think of a more thorough way to crush a man's ego than to belittle his prowess in bed. With a shudder of self-loathing, she lifted her chin, forcing herself to glare directly into his eyes. She couldn't do it, and focused on his throat. "I fake it very well."

The long, drawn-out silence that followed was more hurtful than a physical blow. At last he growled quietly, "Look me in the eyes and say that."

She felt sick. Nevertheless, in order to keep him at arm's length, she had to make him believe her. She forced herself to meet his gaze. His earthy eyes caught and held hers, pain shimmering in their depths. At the sight she stopped breathing completely.

Though she had opened her mouth to repeat her cruel lie, no words came. Her eyes stung, and she knew in seconds she would burst into tears. His eyes, dark and miserable, impelled her to recant—to admit that she was lying—but the icy fear twisting around her heart helped her hold her tongue. She couldn't allow things to go further between them. Drawing herself up, she drove herself to respond. "You heard me."

She tried to spin away, but couldn't. She seemed to be frozen to the spot, compelled to witness the results of her shabby handiwork, glimmering in his eyes. "Right," he finally said. Though he spoke quietly, his voice held a cold edge of irony. "I'm glad we had this little talk." Kneeling beside his dog, he picked up the brush and began to groom the animal.

Bereft and desolate, Deedee stared at his stony profile. Watched his jaw flex angrily. Terrible regret assailed her and her throat ached to cry out the truth. But she couldn't. Didn't dare. She had to remember her life's goal—to find an eternal kind of love. She had to protect her heart from this fly-by-night cowboy. He was resilient. By next week he wouldn't recall her name, anyway. Yet even realizing that, she still felt like the lowest form of slime.

As she fled, her anguish was like a steel weight in her gut. How could she have told such a nasty lie? She'd intended to rebuff him—to force a wedge between them—but she hadn't anticipated the hurt she would see in his eyes. Rushing into the house, she stumbled blindly into the kitchen, grateful Clara and Perry weren't around to witness her tears. Grabbing a dishcloth, she jammed it against her face to muffle her sobs. She'd never been cruel to anyone before. It was an ugly, vile business, and she wondered if safeguarding her heart was any excuse for such brutality.

SEVERAL HOURS LATER as Deedee set the table for supper, the phone rang. Clara was in the garden, Perry had gone to water the stock and Garth had driven off some time ago. So Deedee answered it. She was startled to discover the call was for her.

"Yes," she said, "This is Deedee Emerson." She was so stunned at the man's next words, she almost dropped the receiver. A major Oklahoma City newspaper was planning to start a local helpful-hints column. And he thought she'd be perfect to write it!

"Oh, yes, I'm sure I could," she said, trying to sound professional and not squeal into the receiver. The way he talked, it was practically a done deal. She would come into his office so that they could discuss salary and when she'd start. "Certainly. Next Wednesday at ten o'clock is fine."

As he heartily welcomed her aboard, she scribbled the address and the time of their appointment on a notepad beside the phone. "I'm looking forward to working with you, Mr. Miller. Yes. Thank you!"

When she hung up, she let out a whoop. A columnist!

On a major Oklahoma daily! And it was in the bag—an absolutely fantastic bag!

She danced a jig, then ran to the front door, flinging it open. "Garth!" she called, dying to share the news with him. Then she remembered, and her smile faded. He was gone. He'd left after her cruel pronouncement about his sexual ability, and who could blame him?

He hadn't taken his things, or his dog. And his horse trailer was still parked beside the house. He'd be back. He was running errands, or checking on his own ranch out by Keystone Lake. She inhaled, experiencing a distressing combination of elation and depression.

Darn Garth anyway, for being gone and taking the bang out of her news. Darn him for driving her to insult him and making her feel guilty about it. Darn his lips and his smile and his scent for the hypnotic effect they had on her— making her want things that she knew were no good for her. Darn his kisses and his body and the marvelous way those gentle, knowing hands...

She sank to the couch, trying not to think about the sexy things she didn't dare allow herself to experience, ever again. "I'd better get that job," she muttered between clenched teeth. "I have to get that job!"

AT BREAKFAST the next morning Deedee and Garth played a very good game of "polite acquaintances" for Clara and Perry. Though Garth laughed and talked as though nothing had happened between them, Deedee could see a difference in his eyes. When their glances met, the amusement in the rich, brown depths had disappeared, replaced by a remoteness that chilled her.

She breathed a sigh when breakfast was over, though Garth stubbornly lingered at his place, sipping the last of his coffee. Since it had become Deedee's job to clear the table, she hurriedly began. After taking a batch of dishes to the kitchen, where Clara ran wash water in the sink, she reluctantly reentered the dining room, knowing she and Garth would be alone.

He glanced up as she entered, his long lashes and sultry eyes a disarming sight no matter how many times she looked at them. His coffee mug was poised at his lips. For a few foolish seconds she found herself unable to tear her gaze from those eyes, her pulse beat increasing. Only when Garth looked away, swallowing the last of his coffee, was she able to move.

He pushed back from the table and Deedee went on gathering dishes, though her hands trembled.

The ringing of the telephone almost made her scream, and it took a valiant effort to keep from flinging plates in all directions.

"I'll get it," Garth called.

Deedee was nearly through the kitchen door when he murmured, "It's for you."

He'd spoken too quietly for his grandparents to hear. She halted, startled. Was this another job offer? Maybe things weren't as desperate as she'd feared. Excitement gave her a lightness of step as she set the dishes on the table and dashed to the phone. Unable to meet his eyes, she focused on his shirtfront as she took the receiver from his hand. "Thanks," she murmured. "Hello?"

She was startled to hear Mr. Miller's voice on the line. He sounded hesitant today, and a tinge guilty. He didn't beat around the bush with the bad news.

"Oh—I see...." she breathed, her hopes crushed. "The job's been filled. I—I understand. Of course." Yes, she understood. It was all too clear. The long arm of the DeWinter family had reached out and strangled her chances—even as far away as Oklahoma City. "Yes—yes…you're very kind…."

He hung up, and for some reason, she couldn't deal with the fact that he'd so abruptly broken the connection. "Goodbye, Mr. Miller," she murmured into the dead phone. Her mind cried, *Please don't let this be true! Please come back on the line, tell me it was all a mistake! A bad joke!*

But it wasn't a mistake. It was bad, but it was no joke. Mr. Miller had hung up, and he would never call back. Fighting tears, she replaced the receiver in its cradle. Before she realized she'd moved, she had lowered herself to the couch.

"What happened?" Garth's question startled her. She'd assumed he'd left to check cattle.

Dipping her chin to hide her watery eyes, she shook her head. "Nothing. It seems the job's—" Her voice caught and she couldn't go on.

"It's been filled," he finished.

She nodded, positive he would feel vindicated. Maybe it was karma that this should happen. She didn't deserve a great job, not after what she'd said to him yesterday.

"Do you believe it?"

She tried to respond, but the "no" came out with a choked sob. Instead she twisted her hands in her lap, shaking her head.

"Nice bunch, the DeWinters," he muttered, dark sarcasm in his tone.

She sniffed, struggling to keep from crying.

"I'm sorry," he finally said, very softly.

She glanced up at him, wiping at a tear with the back of her hand. He'd put on his Stetson. His eyes were shadowed, but his face was lined with concern. She found herself believing he meant it. "Thanks." With the heel of her hand, she brushed away another tear, forcing back her despair. This was only one telephone call. Just one rejection. So what if it had been a great job? There were other great jobs out there. She'd mailed over thirty letters. There was no need to be devastated. Vaulting up, she straightened her spine and strode to the table. "Well, these dishes won't do themselves."

"Why don't you come with me this morning," he offered.

She stilled, peering at him.

He shrugged. "A horseback ride in the country air might help."

She hesitated, knowing that going anywhere alone with Garth wasn't the brightest idea in the world. But she felt awful. And he was right. One thing about growing up on the ranch that hadn't been so terribly, terribly bad had been riding her horse—galloping along the hills and hollows, feeling free and alive. She gulped, shifting a fork from one plate to another. A ride in the country would be nice, but with Garth?

"I won't lay a hand on you," he murmured.

She shot him a questioning look, wondering if he'd read her mind. His eyes were gentle, understanding. Irresistible.

He lifted his hands as though in surrender. "I promise."

Straightening, she nodded, but couldn't quite smile. "Thanks. I think that might help."

He winked, as though in encouragement, but his expression remained serious. "Grandma," he shouted. "Deedee's coming with me to count cattle."

Clara appeared in the dining room doorway, tying an apron around her middle. She smiled broadly, looking as though she couldn't think of a thing she'd like better than to see the two of them going off together. "Now there's an idea." Patting Deedee on the shoulder, she said, "Take my little mare, Breezy. And you two have a grand time."

As they headed outside, Garth held the kitchen door for Deedee, allowing her to precede him. He smelled especially good this morning, and she found herself inhaling appreciatively. A warning voice in her head buzzed like an irritating gnat: *"You've agreed to go for a ride in the country with Garth Gentry? The Pollinator? Just the two of you and a few unarmed cows? Deedee Emerson, have you gone insane?"*

# 9

CLOUDS GATHERED and the day became as gloomy as Deedee's mood. She and Garth rode along in an atmosphere of strained quiet while he checked the mama cows and their calves. Luckily, all was well with the cattle.

Without asking her opinion, Garth led her deeper and deeper into the Gentry property. She didn't mind, really. The scenery was lovely. The rolling hills were overlaid with tall grasses and red and yellow splashes of Indian paintbrush. Oaks, elms and a few towering pecans presided over spatterings of deep shade. The two of them skirted a meandering creek, murmuring and giggling in a shadowy hollow.

The breeze picked up, ushering in cooler air. It felt good after days and days of hot, dry weather. Deedee inhaled, her body and soul beginning to calm and heal under nature's gentle solace.

She scanned the pastureland spread out in a panorama before her. As her gaze roved, her attention fell on Garth, riding slightly ahead of her. He sat his cutting horse with relaxed grace, as though he and his stallion were one mighty entity. Of course, to win all those championships he'd almost need to have a psychic link with the animal, so she shouldn't have been surprised that they were in such obvious sync.

That thought summoned unwanted images into her mind's eye, reminding her of how marvelously she and

Garth had been in sync the other night. Unsettled, she dropped her gaze to her hands, clutching the reins of Clara's sorrel mare. Why couldn't she keep those hot visions from her mind for one whole minute?

"What did you say your horse's name was?" she blurted, hoping to shift her thoughts to a less inflammatory topic.

After a few seconds he turned, his expression grave. "Doc's Candy Man," he said. "Candy Man, for short." He turned away.

She knew he was having second thoughts about inviting her along. Considering everything, she was hardly surprised that he didn't have much to say to her.

She scanned his horse, which was the same rich brown as Garth's eyes. Candy Man? That name brought back a flood of rich sensations—erotic memories of how sweet Garth tasted—and she stifled a groan. *Candy Man, of all things.* Ironies ran rampant, or was it only her twisted thought processes at work? "Uh—tell me about your ranch?" She hoped this time he'd engage her in more than a one-sentence conversation.

He peered her way, his brows dipping. "What ranch?"

Now it was her turn to be confused. "Yours—out on Keystone."

One corner of his mouth lifted in a half grin, his expression more cynical than amused. "I don't own a ranch, Dee. I have thirty acres overlooking the lake, mainly woods. Besides Candy Man here, I own a few broodmares, and I have one full-time employee." He glanced away. "Then there's my saddle-making workshop. It's built onto my house."

She was startled. "But I thought…"

He eyed her for a second. "I decided a long time ago ranching wasn't for me. So I trained cutters and entered competitions."

"You don't train them any longer?"

He shook his head. "Lost interest. So now I put old Candy Man here out to stud." He patted the horse's neck. "Money's good, and I figure he deserves some fun after all the championships he won for us."

Again she was startled. "That's how you make your living?"

He nodded. "And the saddle business."

She found herself fighting a grin, and when he next glanced her way, his eyes narrowed. "What's funny?"

"You're a horse's *pimp?*"

A dark brow rose. "Excuse me?"

She lifted her chin in a teasing rebuke, finding this side of Garth very interesting. "You heard what I said." She grinned, adding flippantly, "You're a horseflesh peddler!"

His brows dipped, but he didn't appear especially angry. "You think you're funny?"

She nodded. "I think I'm hilarious."

His lips quirked and to Deedee the small softening was a wondrous sight. "Do you want to know what I think?"

She shook her head. "No. I'm fine with what I think, thanks."

"You're fine with what you think, are you?" He lifted his hat and resettled it lower on his brow, scanning her face. She experienced a wayward shiver of appreciation at his close scrutiny, even though the last thing she needed was for Garth to pay close attention to her. "Woman, I hope you're fine with getting swatted on your rear for that slander." He leaped down from his horse and was pulling her off her mount before she could regroup.

She squealed as he dragged her over his shoulder like a sack of feed and began to swat her backside. His touch was playful, without pain. "Who's peddling horseflesh?" he asked.

"You are, you brute!" She tried to cover her bottom with her hands, but he kept pushing them away. "How dare you! Quit that!" she yelled, but the laughter in her voice told a whole other story. "You're a Neanderthal!"

"So I'm a Neanderthal now?"

"Absolutely!" she retorted, forcing crispness into her tone. "You're a horse pimp and—*hey!*"

Abruptly, he lowered her to her back and was straddling her before she could open her eyes. When she blinked up at him, her laughter froze in her throat. He'd lost his Stetson and his hair was attractively mussed. Though he wasn't touching her, his hands were close to her body, his fingers splayed on the grass near her breasts. His eyes glowed with both humor and desire. "You'd better think real hard," he warned in a seductive drawl. "Do you take back what you said or are you prepared to suffer the consequences?"

She felt an unbidden quiver of anticipation. She lay beneath him, yet his body didn't touch hers. A disobedient need suddenly overpowered her. She *wanted* to suffer whatever consequences he might have in mind—as long as it involved touching, front to front. "What..." she began, then had to clear the dryness from her throat. "What consequences?"

He bent closer, his lips slightly parted. Tempting, enticing. "The consequences are I make love to you." The amusement had vanished from his gaze. He was all serious business now, whetted and waiting.

She watched his nostrils flare, and she understood what he was doing. He was daring her to deny again what they'd shared. He was provoking her to say the same ugly thing she'd said yesterday—or to admit that she was a dirty, rotten liar.

"My lovemaking *would* be disagreeable," he murmured, his eyes impaling her. "Wouldn't it, Dee?"

She felt the sexual magnetism that made him so irresistible radiating from him, heating her body. He held himself above her, his gaze roving over her face, her throat, her breasts....

She stared, trying to keep her longing from showing in her face. When their eyes met again, his were filled with fierce sparks. "Well?" he demanded, making her jump. "What is it to be? Do you take back what you said?" His head dipped a fraction lower, and he challenged in a low growl, "Or do you take back what you said?"

His resolute gaze bored into her in silent calculation. A prickling began in the pit of her stomach. Her heart jolted and her pulse thundered. Logic counseled her to admit nothing, crawl away, mount her horse and gallop madly back to the house. Yet her heart cried out for something entirely different—for a tearful admission and the joyous touch of his lips, his hands, his body.

Hysteria like she'd never known before welled up inside her. What should she do? Her emotions in turmoil, she looked away, squirmed restlessly, clutching tufts of grass in her fists.

"Dee," he breathed, his tone husky with warning and something else. Was it yearning? Was he suffering, too? "Tell me."

What would he do if she took back her ugly lie? Would he laugh and say, "I knew it," leap on his horse and race home to carve another notch in his bedpost? Did he think that once she admitted her lie, everything would be all right? That they would make wild love right here in the grass, among the flowers, under God's own sky? Is that what he thought? Expected? Wanted?

And what about her? What did she want?

*Him! You want him!*

"Okay—okay," she cried, shoving logic aside, her emotions taking command. Her guilt had been eating her alive since the moment she'd lied to him. She couldn't stand it one second longer. "I take it back."

His gaze fixed on her face, he clenched and unclenched his jaw. "Which?"

Her tears of shame blurred his strong, intent features. "Both," she cried in a whisper. "I—I take it back—about both...." Choking on a sob, she reached up, impulsively encircling his neck with her arms. She couldn't help herself. This was the last thing she wanted—but, damn her, she had no control over how she felt.

Running her hands through the soft hair at his nape, she cherished the feel of it, cherished the texture and scent of his skin, the taut muscles of his shoulders. She loved this man—she couldn't deny it any longer—and she couldn't lie about it, not even to save herself from a broken heart.

He might not own a ranch—a pleasant revelation—but he was still The Pollinator, with no interest in being a one-woman man. Unfortunately for her, it was too late to be rational or sensible. Right now she only knew she couldn't deny him anything. She was a fool and she wasn't lying to herself about that, either. What came later would just have to come.

"Kiss me, Garth," she breathed. "Love me...."

Much later, they lay entangled in each other's arms. Garth had spread his shirt on the grass and Deedee lay on it, snuggled in the crook of his arm. Kissing his chest, she relished the powerful beat of his heart against her lips.

He had made love to her so tenderly and thoroughly, she didn't believe she would ever be able to stand again. Right now she didn't care, and smiled, closing her eyes. His hand at her waist drew her more intimately against him. "You're not going to sleep on me, are you, Dee?"

"Umm."

His deep laughter rumbled through her. "Is that a yes or a no?"

She splayed her fingers over his hard belly. "What was the question?"

He bent to kiss the top of her head. "Never mind. Sleep if you want to."

She felt brand-new, whole. Curling her arms about him, she inhaled his scent, mixed with that of green grass and distant rain. "Garth, since your ex-wife, hasn't there been a woman you've liked enough to chase after?" She bit her tongue. Where had that question come from? Making a face, she squeezed her eyes shut. "Sorry. None of my business."

He stroked the small of her back. "It's okay. But the answer's no. I'm not cut out for the long haul."

Her heart constricted. "Are you sure?"

He shifted and she could tell he was looking down at her. "I'm sure." His hand moved to her stomach and he pressed her to her back, so that he could see her face. "You're not getting serious on me, are you, sugar?"

She cringed inwardly at the use of "sugar." He was already distancing himself, even as he kissed her nose, then lightly brushed her lips with his own. "I don't make commitments when I know someday I'll break them."

She struggled to keep her features poised, though her throat ached with despair. "That's—that's probably wise."

He kissed her lips again, and in spite of her dismal mood, she thrilled at his touch. Clearly, she was the queen of all fools. "Garth," she exclaimed, a sudden, heartening thought striking her. "How long have you had your dog?"

He squinted at her, his smile crooked. "You want to talk about my dog right now?"

She lifted a shoulder in what she hoped looked like a casual shrug. "How long?"

He ran his tongue along her collarbone, making her tremble. "Thirteen years, give or take," he murmured.

A delicious shudder warmed her body, and she fought a need to shove him to his back and climb on top. "What would you do if he got lost?"

"I'd look for him." His kisses began to burn across the rise of her breast.

"How long would you look?"

"Until I found him."

"Because you love him, right?"

He stopped kissing her and looked at her. "What?"

She smiled at his charming distraction. Heat glittered in his eyes as he tried to make love to her while she insisted on talking about his dog. "You love Dawg, don't you? And you've loved him for thirteen years?"

Garth ran a hand through his hair. "Yeah."

"And your grandparents? You've loved them all your life? And your horse? You love your horse?"

He nodded. "Yeah. And I'd like to get on with loving you." He nipped at her earlobe. "If we're done with questions."

His hand slid down below her belly to invade her womanly core, and she gasped. "Okay..." she agreed, sighing. "No—no more questions."

What good would it do to try to explain, anyway? He refused to see that if he could love a scroungy old mutt for thirteen years, he had everything it took to love a woman—forever. If he wouldn't let himself understand that his ex-wife hadn't been the right mate for him, it was hopeless trying to force him to see it. Convincing somebody who didn't want to be convinced was impossible. She'd learned that lesson trying to talk sense to her father.

"Oh, Garth...." she moaned. Her soul-deep wretchedness dimmed as he coaxed from her bright, new wellsprings of desire. All other thoughts ebbing away, she eagerly met him kiss for kiss, caress for caress, loving him recklessly and without hope.

How could a few hours change everything so drastically? Clara and Perry had driven to Tulsa to see their doctor. An hour ago, they'd called with the news that Perry's arm was fine. And by a stroke of dumb luck, they'd met a Catoosa man at the doctor's getting the stitches removed from a cut on his forehead. He'd just been laid off at the feed store. Since Perry and Clara had known the shy young man for years, they'd given him the ranch-hand job on the spot. He would start tomorrow.

So Garth was heading home this afternoon.

Deedee sat on the front steps, feeling empty and lost. She wondered sadly if she would have been better off marrying Ty. He would have given her a secure life. After all, she had been fond of him. Most importantly of all, she would never have met Garth Gentry—the carefree rogue who had no use for her other than as a temporary plaything.

She inhaled, then quickly exhaled, sick at heart. If Garth remembered her at all, it would be as "that woman I had while Grandpa was in the splint." The realization was enough to make her want to bang her fists against a brick wall until they were bleeding and broken. In a matter of moments Garth would hop in his truck and, without a backward glance, leave her coughing in his exhaust.

Adding insult to injury, she'd received six responses to her resumé that day informing her there were no jobs available. And if she wasn't getting rejection letters, her resumés were being ignored, for the phone wasn't ringing, either.

She tried not to watch as Garth loaded Candy Man into his trailer. Picking up the pliers in her lap, she turned her attention to Dawg. "Okay, sweetie." She scratched him between the ears. "Don't be afraid, this won't hurt." She felt along his coat, locating a spiny cocklebur. Clamping down on it with the pliers, she crushed it. Moving her hand again, she found another burr, repeating the act. "Wherever you went today, don't go back. You're a mess." *He won't,* her mind goaded, *he's leaving today—with Garth.* The reminder was like a knife twisting inside her. Pursing her lips, she adjusted her glasses and continued her search for burrs.

As she worked, she heard the Gentrys' old sedan rumbling along the drive. It had rained during lunch, so no dust was kicked up by their arrival. She did her best to look casual as she waved the pliers at them.

Perry waved back with his right arm, proving that he was truly healed. She watched them clamber out of their car and zero in on Garth. Deedee didn't listen to their conversation, their voices were indistinct and soft, except for Perry's. He boomed a hearty goodbye to his grandson.

She lifted her gaze, unable to stop herself, and watched Garth hug his grandmother and then his granddad. She experienced a twinge of jealousy for the special place the old couple held in his life. The joy of being held tenderly in his arms would haunt her for a long, long time. With a despondent sigh she turned to Dawg. "It looks like it's about time to go. I guess I'd better hurry."

Perry and Clara shuffled up the steps. "Always working." Clara laughed. "I'm not even going to ask what you're doing." She patted Deedee's shoulder. "Once Garth leaves, come on in. I bought the makin's for ice cream. Figured we'd celebrate Pa's return to the world of the two-handed." She bent lower, adding, "Besides, now *he* can work the crank."

Deedee nodded, manufacturing a grin, but her heart wasn't in it. When the couple had gone inside, she turned back to see Garth coming her way. She stiffened, but made herself go back to what she'd been doing. Locating another burr, she crushed it with the pliers.

Garth loped onto the porch. "Don't kill—"

"My dog, sugar," she interjected, without looking up. "I know."

He sat down. Resting a hand on the porch behind her, he leaned her way. "What are you doing?" Amusement rode his voice.

She held her breath, trying not to inhale his scent. Smoothing her fingers along Dawg's fur, she made herself go on with what she'd been doing. "I'm crushing burrs," she said, too breathlessly for her liking. "They're easy to comb out once they're crushed."

He chuckled. "I've got to go. I'll brush him out at home." Leaning close, he kissed her cheek. "Thanks, though."

Deedee nodded, but refused to meet his eyes, fearing he'd see too much in hers. "You're welcome."

She could hear him move to stand and was startled when he took her hand, tugging her up. "I hate to say goodbye to you." He smiled, his eyes soft. Her heart fluttered with wild hope until his grin turned teasing. "I've never met a woman who could muck out a stall the way you can."

The blow was hard and directly between the eyes, but she managed to lift her chin, hiding her bitter disappointment. "I've never met a man who could throw bull as far as you can."

Garth's laugh was rich and mellow. The sound tormented her, for she would never hear it again. His smile faltered, his glance growing circumspect. "Look, Dee, drop me a line when you get settled." His lips lifted encouragingly, but without conviction. "Okay?"

*I'd hope to be damned to a purgatory for fools if I did*

*any such thing, Garth Gentry!* Did he think she was a naive twelve-year-old and couldn't see that he was brushing her off? She pasted on a smile. "Sure," she lied. "Just as soon as I'm settled."

He nodded. "Good." Tugging her close, he kissed her. It was quick, shattering and over too soon. Stunned and dizzy, she could only sink to the steps and blink, trying to focus, as he ambled away. When he reached the truck, he whistled for his dog. Deedee was vaguely aware when the mutt licked her hand in a sloppy farewell, then shambled after his master.

Less than a minute later, Garth drove out of her life.

Clara's voice calling from the doorway jerked her from her stupor. "Yes?" She blinked back stupid tears. She'd known Garth would leave her. She just hadn't known it would be today.

She got up, managing a relatively placid expression. "Ready to do the ice cream?" Walking to the door, she was alarmed to discover how heavy her limbs felt. She prayed this mental and physical depression wouldn't last long.

"Almost ready." Clara closed the door behind them. "I called you in because there's a phone call for you."

Deedee stumbled to a halt. "Really?"

Clara smiled, lifting both gnarled hands. Her fingers were crossed. "I hope it's about a job," she said under her breath. "Good luck, honey." Hugging Deedee's shoulders, the older woman scurried into the kitchen, leaving Deedee her privacy.

She was so emotionally drained, she couldn't pick up the receiver until she sat down on the couch. Taking a restorative breath, she lifted it, hoping her voice would sound steadier than she felt. "Hello, this is Deedee Emerson."

"Miss Emerson, this is Oscar Peabody," announced a

hearty, machine-gun-fire voice. "I own the *Mystic Hill Weekly Chieftain.* I got your resumé, and I'm looking for somebody. Has to be just the right person, though. Needs to want to put down roots—buy me out one of these days, when I retire. If you're interested, maybe we can talk. You'd work for me until I retire—maybe six months to a year—then you can start buying me out. It's a little paper, but Mystic Hill's a good spot to live. Just a hop, skip and a jump from Tulsa over here on Keystone Lake."

She sat there stunned, both by the effervescent way the man talked about his offer—not just a job, but a business!—and by the location. Keystone Lake? That was a bit of bad luck. What if she ran into Garth? On the other hand, Keystone was a big lake. It was unlikely he lived near Mystic Hill.

It was a great opportunity. Garth had already taken her heart. Did she dare allow him to ruin what might be her one chance for a career in journalism? "Mr. Peabody, I—I like your proposition very much. However, there's something I must tell you." She decided to put the bad news right there on the table, to avoid more crushing disappointments like the one this morning.

"Tell away, Miss Emerson," he urged boisterously. "And by the way, call me Oscar. Everybody does." He chortled. "Well, truth be told, everybody calls me Old Oscar. So what is it you need to confess? You can't spell?"

She smiled at his outgoing way and his humor. "No, I can spell. And…and please call me Deedee." She counted to ten, then decided it had to be said. "It's just that I—well, I was fired from the *American-Gazette.*"

There was a long pause that Deedee tried to fill by fiddling with the phone cord. She wished he'd hang up and get it over with. "Fired, you say?" Oscar repeated. "What for?"

She swallowed. "Uh—well, I didn't marry Tyler De-Winter."

Another long pause, then snickering that grew louder and louder until it had become riotous guffaws. "You're the little dickens I saw on the news! Sure! Now I remember where I heard that name."

She made a pained face. "Yes, that was me."

"Well, dang it, Deedee!" he said. "Now I *know* I'm going to like you. I was fired from that overpriced rag forty years ago, but I didn't have a great reason like leaving a DeWinter twirp crying at the church." He burst into another bout of snickering. "They fired me for my attitude, so I took my attitude and started my own paper. Met the love of my life, got married and had five kids who all grew up to be doctors and lawyers. Shiftless bunch." He laughed at his joke. "Somewhere along the road I lost the attitude. Now I'm thinking about retiring, and I'd like to see the old *Chieftain* left in good hands. What do you say? Do you want to give it a try?"

She sat there utterly blank, speechless. He didn't mind that she'd been fired!

"Deedee, are you there?"

His question snapped her out of her daze. "I...yes, I'm here, uh, Oscar. Well, if you're sure, I'm willing to give you my very best."

"Heck fire, Deedee, that sounds good to me. We'll call you the assistant managing editor. Since there's only four of us, that means your job'll be to do everything but clean the toilets. And I can't promise it won't come to that. Can you start in a week?"

With tears of gratitude and relief running down her cheeks, she nodded, then realized he couldn't hear that. "Yes—yes. I'll be there." She didn't add that if it ever came to cleaning the toilets, she knew a great household tip for getting rid of unsightly rings.

ONCE HE SWUNG his pickup onto the highway, Garth let out a long, slow breath. This was good. Things would get back to normal now. He was on his way home and Deedee Emerson would find a job and get on with her life.

He sniffed the air. What the hell? He felt a blow in his gut when he realized her scent still clung to his shirt. Damnation. He took some deep breaths, trying to convince his body that there was nothing to be turned on about. But with every breath, her essence filled his head. Talk about a no-win situation.

The bespectacled little woman who made the taste of cigars an aphrodisiac and who bossed him around in bed was gone. Out of his life. And it was fine with him.

Her fragrance wafted up to harass him again. He ground out a blasphemy, rolling down the window to let the rain-scented air dilute her scent. He'd be damned if that little wisp of a female was going to change him in any way. He'd already been married. It didn't take.

Old Dawg lay sprawled on the seat, his head on Garth's thigh. When the dog yawned, Garth glanced at him, then affectionately patted his ribs. "What was she talking about out there, Dawg?" he muttered. "You and my grandparents—and Candy Man?" Mystified, he shook his head. "She's a strange one, that woman."

*Strange, maybe, but exciting,* he found himself admitting silently. Their fling had been spectacu—er, fine. They'd both had a good time, but it was over. His life was okay the way it was. He had enough women without muddying up his perfectly satisfactory existence by getting attached to one—especially one quite so quaint.

*Quaint?* his mind sneered. *Not in bed, she isn't quaint!*

He shifted, his jeans suddenly binding. Okay, so they'd been good together. Maybe very good. Damn her, the bossy, big-eyed mantrap. She flashed into his mind—naked, ripping off his shirt buttons. Sweat broke out on his forehead and he experienced another rush of heaviness in his groin.

"Hell," he muttered, fighting to squelch the saucy vision. "What man worth his salt wants to be bossed around in bed, anyway?"

# 10

JULY WAS LIKE most Julys in eastern Oklahoma—hot and humid. Mystic Hill was a rustic wood-and-brick community of fifteen hundred souls. The sleepy little burg was carved into a hillside overlooking Keystone Lake, so it didn't seem quite so hot to Deedee.

She was elated that the attic apartment she'd found had a lake view—well, if you stood on a chair and looked way over to the left, between Mandy's Café and the barbershop.

The newspaper office's front window had a better view and Deedee never tired of glimpsing sailboats skimming along the placid surface of the man-made lake. Of course, she hardly ever had time to sit and gaze. Her job at the *Chieftain* kept her busy, and she was glad. She needed to keep busy.

In the five weeks she'd worked there, Deedee had become fond of Old Oscar and the two other employees, Lela and Sadie—both spirited matrons twice Deedee's age.

She sensed Oscar was fond of her, as well. They'd already begun reviewing ways to finance her purchase of the paper. Though she would never be rich owning a small weekly, she would have a nice business in a pleasant town. How many people could say as much about their lives?

She was happy with the way things were turning out. At least that's what she tried to believe. Unfortunately, a gaping emptiness inside her couldn't be filled with things like an interesting job, a lovely view or congenial friends.

Garth's memory lingered, leaving no room for romantic thoughts about other men she'd met in Mystic Hill or, she feared, for any man she would ever meet.

She'd been introduced to a few eligible bachelors who were clearly interested in her, men who could offer security and possibly even an eternal kind of love. But she would never know, for the tragic irony was that her heart was no longer hers to give. It belonged to a footloose cowboy whose kisses had branded her for life.

She hadn't seen Garth or heard from him in thirty-six days and two hours, but who was counting? She was thankful their paths hadn't crossed. Why rip open old wounds? Even so, she called Clara weekly, keeping the older woman posted on her job, her apartment, Magnolia and the people she'd met in town. Deedee had grown to love the elderly Gentry couple as though they were her own grandparents. Her feelings about Garth notwithstanding, she refused to lose them, too.

Clara mentioned her grandson from time to time, insisting he only lived "down the road" from Mystic Hill. Deedee knew Clara passed along to Garth every detail of their calls. And since he'd made no attempt, it was painfully clear he didn't plan to get in touch with her.

Deedee shook her head, annoyed with herself. What was she doing wasting her time on dreary, self-pitying thoughts? This was Saturday afternoon. People shouldn't have unhappy thoughts on a Saturday afternoon. She'd promised Magnolia that they'd have chicken livers tonight. She wasn't that crazy about the dish, but Magnolia lived and died for her occasional chicken liver treat. After all, it *was* Saturday. Somebody in the family might as well be deliriously happy on a Saturday night.

She couldn't afford a car quite yet, so Deedee was glad the town's supermarket was only a few blocks from where she lived. When the mechanical doors whooshed open and she stepped inside, the air-conditioning was a welcome relief. Grabbing a cart, she scanned her list.

She couldn't get used to the way everybody knew everybody else in town. It seemed as if each time she turned down another aisle, somebody piped, "Hi Deedee!" or "How's it going, Deedee?" or "How's the newspaper game, Deedee?" She enjoyed the family feel of Mystic Hill, and hoped that soon she'd be able to call everyone by name in return.

"Hi, Dee."

She stilled in the act of placing an onion into a plastic sack. Nobody in the world had ever called her Dee, except...

Her body flashed hot and cold at the same time and her foolish heart soared. Luckily, Garth was behind her, so she had a chance to collect herself before she turned around.

Forcing her fingers to release the onion into the bag, she grabbed a twist tie from the holder. Busying herself tying off the plastic, she faced him. By the time she made eye contact, she felt sure she looked like a person without a care in the world, though her hammering heart was turning her rib cage to dust. "Why, hello, Garth." For a split second she'd toyed with the idea of pretending to forget his name, but she wasn't that good an actress. She smiled and the effort hurt.

He lounged between the cucumbers and cantaloupes. With his hip propped against the counter, he looked like he was posing for a yummy advertisement—the Marlboro Man of the Vegetarian Set. His grin was as devastating as ever, and she steeled herself against it. He pushed back the brim of his hat with his thumb, the move absurdly sexy.

The earthy gaze that tortured her every night in her dreams roamed languidly from her brimmed ball cap patterned with mauve rosebuds to her mauve T-shirt, then traveled down to take in her matching, flared shorts. She had an urge to bolt and run, but refused to humiliate herself with an open display of hysteria.

Though he'd seen her canvas sandals before, his attention lingered on her feet for a disturbing length of time. She wondered why. Was he in the market for summer footwear? Surely he wasn't recalling those shoes lying beside his bed, kicked off in a fit of lusty abandon.

Her chin snapped up at the emotional slap of that memory. Allowing herself to be stared at like some cow on the auction block was ridiculous. "It's nice to have seen you, Garth," she said stiffly, pushing her cart forward. Her intent was to slip quickly past him, but she made it only as far as the cucumbers before his hand on hers thwarted her escape. His touch staggered her.

"You look good, Dee."

*So do you. Too good! Please, let me go, Garth!* "Thank you," she mumbled, meeting his eyes with reluctance. "Now, if you'll excuse—"

"Oh, Garth! There you are!" a high-pitched voice called. He looked up, over Deedee's head. Unable to help herself, she turned. A statuesque brunette pranced their way, pushing a clattering grocery cart half-filled with foodstuffs. The woman wore white, skintight slacks and a red tube top. Her ample breasts jiggled like gelatin as she moved. The woman appeared to be around twenty—tall, golden and pampered looking. She made a face as though frustrated. "Oh, Garth!" she repeated, with a wave. "I asked the butcher and he said they don't sell antelope meat here. Just the regular. You know—beef and chicken and stuff."

Garth laughed, and against her will, Deedee's gaze lifted to his face. "I said cantaloupe, darlin'."

The stranger's high-heeled sandals tap-tap-tapped as she

hastily joined them, her giggle self-conscious. "Cantaloupe! I thought you said to meet you in the *antelope* section." She took his arm possessively and eyed Deedee. "Have we met?" Though her voice was friendly, her eyes warned, *Get away from him, he's mine!*

"Samantha Dice, this is Deedee Emerson," Garth said. "Deedee, Samantha."

They shook hands. Samantha's breasts jiggled and her bracelets jangled.

"I'm new in town." Deedee tried to focus on introducing herself to the jiggly-jangly woman, but she could feel Garth's eyes on her. It was disconcerting.

"The newspaper lady, right?" Samantha asked, but didn't give Deedee time to answer. "My daddy's Dick Dice of Dice Realty." She slipped her hand from Deedee's and curled her fingers around Garth's arm. "You've probably heard his slogan, If You Want a House That's Really Nice, Try Dice. That's Daddy."

"Oh, of course, he advertises in—"

"Garth?" Samantha interrupted. She faced him, her brow puckering. "What did you want cantaloupe for?"

"I like it."

"For dessert?"

He cocked a skeptical brow. "I thought so."

She giggled, slapping his arm coquettishly. "Don't be silly, sweetie. Let's have cheesecake. They sell the best frozen ones here." She pecked his cheek. "I'll get one and you pick up the steaks. I told the butcher to cut some *really* special. See you at the checkout." She pranced away without a glance at Deedee, her cart clattering into the distance.

Concentrating on keeping her breathing even, Deedee made herself scan her list. She had to keep her mind on groceries, though it was impossible with Garth so near. His scent beckoned; his body fairly radiated sexuality, tempting, taunting. Her heart sputtered and lurched like the ruined piece of junk it was. "Well, I guess you'd better get those steaks," she mumbled, hating herself for her foolish need to look at him just once more.

He was watching her, his expression serious, his eyes gentle and somehow sad. "I've missed you, Dee."

*I've missed you, Dee?* He had some colossal nerve. His jangling friend had just jiggled off and he had the brass to suggest he'd missed *Deedee?* She shook her head at him, her lips curling skeptically. "I can tell."

His brows dipped at her sarcasm. "Look," he said, sounding suddenly tense, "I'm busy this evening, but what about a movie tomorrow?"

She was startled by the invitation, then realized she shouldn't be. No doubt he felt he had to ask, and that was the reason for his tenseness. It was probably one of those unwritten guy rules—if you run into someone you've slept with, then dropped like a hot potato, you have to make the offer, however empty. She supposed it was her duty to recognize the invitation as insincere, and decline.

Apparently there was a certain amount of social red tape to being used and dumped these days. She swallowed hard, making a valiant effort to appear nonchalant. They might as well get the formalities over and done with so she could try and get on with her life. "Thanks, but I'm busy," she lied.

He squinted slightly and there was a vague sideways movement of his jaw. The expression could have been relief, but it was too brief to read well. "That's a shame," he murmured. "I was going to ask you to marry me—sugar."

Her gaze rocketed to his. He winked, his lips easing into a smile.

Did he have to rub it in? A raw, ferocious anger overwhelmed her. How dare he be so flippant! She supposed she should have expected it, since he asked every women he met to marry him.

Renewed hysteria welled inside her and she laughed out loud. "Of course you were. Why should I be any different?" Her emotions going haywire, she grabbed a cucumber from the display and jabbed it hard into his solar plexus. "Put slices of this on your eyelids. It'll help get rid of the red puffiness from crying."

.He grabbed the vegetable in self-defense. "That's a no, right?" The question came out somewhat winded from the blow to his gut. "Look, Dee—"

"Garth, I have to go," she interrupted, blinking back tears. "Have a nice life."

THE AFTERNOON DRAGGED in spite of the fact that Monday was their second busiest day at the *Chieftain* office. Tuesday was their busiest, when they put the paper to bed. Deedee sat with a hip propped on a tall stool as she pored over the layout pages for this week's edition. Saturday's run-in with Garth loomed in her brain, but she shoved it away. She had to finish this edition of the newspaper, her fifth. She tried to make every edition she worked on better than the last, but to do that she had to keep her mind on her job, not on Garth Gentry.

The usual ads were waxed and stuck in place, and most of the articles were written and printed out in the appropriate column format. Things were proceeding well in spite of the fact that her attention was badly divided.

She called over her shoulder, "Lela, it looks like we're going to have about five column inches to fill on page four. Check the filler board." She turned to face the woman who was sitting at a cluttered desk nearby, chewing on her pen. Deedee had a thought. "What about the band contest story?

It's about the right length, and we've had several of the parents wanting to know when it's going to be in.''

"Sounds good to me," Lela chirped, sticking the chewed end of the pen behind her ear. "You'd think third-runner-up marching bands in Pawnee County wouldn't be that big a deal, but some parents…!" She jumped up to check the wall where they displayed filler stories, already waxed and printed out in column form. Lela squinted at the array of articles. "That Mrs. Winterbothom calls so often you'd think her little Winthrop won the Congressional Medal of Honor." Finding the story, she peeled it off. "The kid plays the *triangle,* for corn's sake."

Deedee laughed. She enjoyed Lela's bantering. A chunky woman thrice divorced, in her mid-fifties, Lela wore a knot of tangerine hair twisted on the crest of her head. She joked all the time and she chewed pens all the time. Everybody's pens suffered; she was an equal-opportunity chewer.

Lela handed the sticky column of text to Deedee. "Here ya go."

"Thanks." Still grinning, Deedee turned back to study the page layouts. "And Sadie, I need the rest of the church news. How's that coming?"

A fortyish widow, Sadie unfailingly came to work in one seventies-era polyester pantsuit or another, always looking like she'd blown in on a windstorm. But she was a grammar and spelling genius, and covered local church and sporting events with equal zeal. "I'm printing it out now," she said, her voice deceptively deep for a woman of five foot one. "Half a minute."

"Great." Deedee slid off the stool and moved down the long, slanted art table to scan pages five and six. "We still need the Founder's Day schedule of events. That has to be in this week's edition. Who's supposed to bring that by?"

"Will I do, sugar?"

Deedee's heart did an ungainly flip-flop. In utter shock she twisted around to see Garth standing there. He held his Stetson in one hand and an envelope in the other. "I returned a repaired saddle to Andy Banks and he asked me to bring this by, as long as I was coming anyway." He held out the envelope.

Lela scurried over. "I'll take it, Garth." She beamed up at him. "Are you getting handsomer or am I getting hornier?"

Garth laughed, slinging an arm about the well-padded woman. "I know a trick question when I hear one, darlin'."

Lela poked him in the chest with her chewed pen. "Well, sweetie-pie, since I can't get any hornier, I guess you're getting handsomer." She took the envelope and waved it at Deedee. "I'll type this into the computer."

Deedee tried to say thanks but her throat was too dry. She cleared it, trying again. "Uh—good, Lela..." She inhaled, the effort thready. "What—what can we do for you, Garth?"

When he aimed his sexy smile at her, it threatened to be her undoing. "I have business with Old Oscar."

She felt a stab of disappointment and couldn't help blurting, "I'm the assistant managing editor. I can take care of any needs you have." She bit the inside of her cheek. That hadn't come out quite the way she'd intended.

He reached up, pressing her glasses more securely into place for her. "I know you can, sugar." The look in his eyes, his sultry tone, cruelly provoked memories of needs they'd satisfied for each other—needs she dared not dwell on. When he dropped his hand, he shoved it in his hip pocket. "But I've done business with Old Oscar for a long time, so I'd just as soon talk to him. Is he in?"

The bridge of her nose sizzled where his flesh had brushed hers. She readjusted her glasses, surreptitiously rubbing away the feel of his touch. Though his nearness unsettled her, she was annoyed that he couldn't spend even five minutes with her about an advertisement for his saddle-making business or his horse pimping or whatever. She jerked her head toward the opposite side of the room and Oscar's private office. "I'm sure you know where to go," she said.

His brows rose and she had a feeling he'd read a double meaning into her comment. Which meant he was a bright lad. He coughed slightly, and she didn't know if it was to cover a laugh or a grunt of discomfiture. "Thanks." He turned away. With a nod to Lela and Sadie, who gawked like schoolgirls, he murmured, "Ladies." Then he disappeared into Oscar's inner sanctum.

Sadie was the first to come to. "That man's a hunk."

Lela giggled. "If I were twenty years younger, he could slip those size eleven's under my bed anytime." With a wistful sigh, she opened the envelope and began to enter the Founder's Day schedule into her computer.

Fidgety, Deedee pressed her hands to her stomach. Why did Garth have to come here? *Probably because it's the only newspaper in town, stupid!* she reminded herself crossly. His scent hovered like an indolent ghost bent on haunting her. She escaped to the rear of the office, into the tiny kitchen that also served as a darkroom. Behind the partition, developing chemicals permeated the air, mingling with the strong, bitter smell of coffee.

Deedee grabbed her assigned mug, pouring herself a cup. She knew that, in her agitated state, caffeine was about the last thing she needed. But she filled her mug, anyway. Slumping against the tile counter, she sipped the steaming brew.

Massaging her temples, she fought the beginnings of a headache. Funny how it had come on so suddenly. Just seeing him standing there, smiling down at her, had done terrible and wonderful things to her insides. She might as well face the fact that she was a sick puppy where Garth Gentry was concerned, and no matter how little he cared for her, getting over him was going to take time. Maybe a lot of time. She counted to ten, trying to calm herself. Then she counted to one hundred, absently sipping the coffee. It didn't work. She wasn't calm.

"Deedee, I've got that Founder's Day schedule printed out in a three-by-five box, the way you wanted."

Deedee rubbed the back of her neck and straightened, carrying her mug into the main room. "Good." She attempted a smile, inhaling to get her emotions on track. "Wax it for me, Lela, and I'll paste it in."

"Check."

Deedee wandered listlessly to the art table. Her heart wasn't into finishing this week's edition. Her heart was in Garth's back pocket—right beside his crumpled bandanna.

She heard a click and realized Garth was coming out of Oscar's office. The older man's guffaw boomed. "It's great to see you, Gentry. You don't get into town enough."

"Good to see you, Oscar. And you'll handle that for me?"

"Consider it done. Consider it done."

"Thanks."

Deedee tried not to listen, not to notice that Garth was there at all. But she couldn't help thinking dark thoughts about men and their dratted good-ol'-boys-club mentality. Old Oscar always took sole possession of pages one and two. He didn't even *do* advertisements anymore. But Garth couldn't force himself to deal with anybody but another man.

Or…was it possibly just *her* that he didn't want to deal with? The thought made her stomach churn. Of course, that had to be it. An infinite sorrow descended over her soul at the realization. He couldn't even stand to be near her for five minutes.

When she felt a nudge on her arm, she jumped, sloshing coffee over the front of her white knit blouse and coral jumper. "Oh, no!" She couldn't believe her bad luck. Black coffee ran down her front, staining her outfit—and Garth Gentry was bearing humiliating witness to it all.

"I'm sorry," Lela cried, jerking the waxed schedule out of harm's way. "I didn't mean to startle you."

Deedee swiped at the coffee, making futile attempts to deflect the liquid before it soaked in. A few seconds later, a wad of paper towels was thrust at her. "Here," Garth said. "This might help."

She grabbed the towels, avoiding eye contact. "Thanks," she mumbled, her body trembling with humiliation.

She rubbed, but did more damage than good. What was the matter with her? Why couldn't she think of the remedy for coffee stains? There was one, but her mind would *not* call it up, apparently too preoccupied with shrieking, *Garth is watching! Garth is watching!* She knew that already, and hearing it ranted over and over inside her skull was not helping the situation.

Trying to hide her mental collapse from the others, she kept wiping, praying Garth would go. But darn the man, he just stood there. Finally, ready to scream, she stopped her useless rubbing and glared at him. "Did you want the towels back, or something?"

He towered in front of her, his arms loosely crossed over his chest. "No." Reaching out, he brushed a drop of coffee from her cheek. At the contact an errant quiver danced along her spine. "I just wanted to say thanks."

She eyed him warily. "For what?"

He looked windswept and casually gorgeous. His smile was casually gorgeous, too, and the sight set off a wayward glow in her middle.

"That cucumber thing worked." He leaned down until their lips were little more than a hand's width apart, his glinting gaze paralyzing her. "My eyes aren't red and puffy. See?" he whispered.

His wink shut off her ability to breathe. When her numbed brain finally kicked in again, Garth Gentry had left the building.

WEDNESDAYS WERE "reward day" at the paper given that Tuesday nights the harried staff put the paper to bed. Today it was Deedee's turn to bring the reward: doughnuts. She was proud to have a whole month and a half of *Chieftains* under her belt. Today, number six was hitting the post office. Subscribers would have it in the morning.

Last night had been unusual for Deedee. Usually she was in the office late into the night, dealing with all the hair-tearing last-minute details. But she'd been assigned to cover the Crappie Queen Pageant, the crowning glory of Founder's Day. It was on Tuesday night this year, since the town council insisted that Founder's Day be celebrated on the actual day, not the nearest weekend. That complication made it harder for the *Chieftain* to get the story into this week's paper, but Oscar had been adamant.

So with her camera and notepad in hand, Deedee had worked the pageant. She'd found herself inordinately gratified when Samantha Dice wasn't crowned Crappie Queen, but came in fourth runner-up. Strangely, Deedee had been inordinately upset that she hadn't caught a glimpse of Garth among the celebrants.

She tried not to think about that. It had been nine days since she'd seen him in the newspaper office, when he'd insisted on talking to Oscar. Garth was out of her life now, so it was time she forced him out of her thoughts. She had to begin accepting dates with the nice bachelors who'd been calling.

And she would, she vowed, as she pushed open the door to the doughnut shop. The place smelled wonderful—of gourmet coffee and freshly baked pastries. Most of the tiny, metal tables were occupied with townsfolk enjoying breakfast and coffee. Many were reading this week's paper, which the doughnut shop carried meaning these folks got an earlier peek than subscribers.

Last night, after the pageant, Deedee had made it back to the newspaper office by ten-thirty. She'd written the story and developed the pictures while Oscar handled the final proofing of the paper. As usual, he held exclusive dominion over the front page. He'd told her how many column inches he needed for the story, and what size to make the photo of this year's Crappie Queen. Deedee had done it all by eleven-thirty.

When she'd handed him the waxed story and photo, Oscar shooed her home along with Lela and Sadie. He'd insisted he could finish up. Though Deedee had protested, he'd practically shoved her out the door.

She yawned now, walking to the doughnut shop's counter. If Oscar only knew that she hardly slept, anyway—what with Garth's teasing smile and sexy body invading her dreams. She could have stayed and put the paper to bed all by herself. For once, it would have been a constructive reason to stay awake.

"Hi, Babs." She smiled tiredly. "How about a dozen twists to go? Two chocolate covered. And a cup of coffee."

Babs nodded, then grinned oddly. "Sure." A short woman with prominent teeth and a dusting of freckles across her nose, she poured a steaming cup, then gestured with the coffeepot toward the stack of newspapers. "Have one on the house."

Deedee laughed. "Now, Babs, don't go giving away our profit."

The young woman giggled. "It's on me." Babs smiled again, then covered her mouth to stifle another giggle. Deedee wondered what had gotten into her. Normally she was pretty blasé. And she *never* mentioned the newspaper.

"Morning, Deedee," somebody called. "Read the paper yet?"

She turned and grinned. "I wrote most of it."

Somebody else chimed in. "Front page is mighty interesting this week."

There were several titters of laughter from surrounding tables, and Deedee scanned the room, puzzled. Everyone was staring at her, big smiles on their faces. Was Babs spiking the coffee with booze today?

"Thanks. I wrote the Founder's Day story." She turned back to the man who had just spoken. She knew his name—Jack, or was it Jake? Darn, when would she get everybody straight?

"Not the story—the ad," Babs said, returning with her boxed order.

"Ad?" Deedee was confused. Oscar never put ads on the front page. Leaning over so that she could reach the end of the counter, she grabbed a paper. Right under the *Chieftain* banner was her lead story, with a photo of this year's smiling Crappie Queen. "What ad?" As she flipped the paper over to look at the lower half of the page, she heard more tittering and whispering.

Her glance caught on a large box of copy in the middle of the front page. "My goodness," she murmured. "There is an ad...." This was diametrically opposed to Oscar's usual policy. Was he having a breakdown?

She scanned it. Her mouth sagged open and she grew still. What did it say? She read the words again, printed in large, bold type, then reread them several more times, trying to decipher their meaning. But every time she read them, they seemed to say the same thing.

"Marry me, Dee. I never met a woman who could muck out a stall the way you can." It was signed simply, "Garth."

Nearby sniggering brought her head up, and she jerked around to stare at the grinning, pointing townspeople. They were having a fine old time at her expense. How dare Garth embarrass her so badly? She had a new job in a new town, and she was trying to make a place for herself. How could he humiliate her and undermine her professional competence this way?

Mucking out stalls, of all things to ridicule her about. If he'd wanted to shame her in front of the whole town, he couldn't have thought of a more thorough way to do it.

Slamming her money on the counter, she barreled out of the store. Down the block at the newspaper office, she confronted Old Oscar, the only one there this early. "Why? Why did you go along with this?" she cried, shaking the newspaper in his face.

"Why, Deedee, child, I think it's romantic," he said with a wide grin.

"Romantic?" She flung her arms up in the air, tossing the paper away. "Have you lost your mind? Don't you know Garth Gentry well enough to know he's a terminal tease? We've never even been on a date!" She dragged her hands through her hair. "How can I show my face in this town? He's made me a laughingstock! Mucking out stalls, for heaven's sake!"

Lanky and utterly bald, Oscar had the decency to look abashed. "I'm sorry you're upset, Deedee." He patted her shoulder. His gray eyebrows, bushy as woolly caterpillars, crawled together. "My intentions were good. I—"

Her groan became a growl of rage. "We all know what the road to hell is paved with, don't we?"

"Good intentions, I know," he mumbled, shrugging sheepishly. "Maybe you should go talk to him." Oscar's hazel eyes were soft with compassion.

She curled her hands into fists sure she would start to breathe fire in the next minute. Maybe Oscar had a point. If she was going to breathe fire, Garth might as well be the one to get torched. After all, this mess was his fault. "You bet I'll talk to him." She spun toward the door.

"One thing's for sure," Oscar called. "He's either a damn jackass or he's crazy in love with you."

Her indignant laughter stabbed the air. "That's a no-brainer!" She slammed out the door. After two seconds she exploded back inside. "Oscar, can I use your car?" Her fury all but choking her, she added, "And where does the jackass live?"

# 11

———————

DEEDEE REMEMBERED something her dad used to say when he was really angry. "Deedee, honey, I'm mad enough to eat the devil with his horns on." As she turned off the road onto Garth's property, she was that mad. The fifteen-minute drive hadn't cooled her off one iota. She was going to take a bite out of Garth right where it hurt, the rotten bum.

Oscar's compact sedan made quick work of traveling Garth's blacktop drive. His house came into view—a long, low ranch style made of raw timber and rock. Nestled among towering blackjack oaks, it looked picturesque and peaceful. Off to the right, Keystone Lake sparkled in the morning sun. On the left, in a cleared area, were his stables built from the same timber and rock as the house. Behind a pole fence, in a pasture, were several horses.

It was a pretty place. Too bad she was going to kill its owner. She slammed on her brakes when she reached the front. Throwing open the car door, she leaped out. The double entry doors of the house were rustic in design. She pounded, ignoring the doorbell.

When a man answered, she had her mouth open to start shouting before she realized it wasn't Garth. She faltered, swallowed. "Uh—is this the Gentry residence?"

The big man was around forty, with a hard jaw, corded neck and swarthy complexion. Wearing a black T-shirt and jeans, he was wiping his hands on a towel. "Yes, ma'am," he said, his bulldog face splitting in a friendly grin that showed off a silver front tooth. "I'm his hired man, Rad. Mr. Gentry's in his workshop." Dawg ambled to the door and poked his scruffy head outside. He gave a bark of greeting—high praise for the laid-back mutt. Rad patted the old dog's head. "I'd take you around, ma'am, but he's got me in the middle of a chore." With a blunt hand, he indicated the side of the house away from the lake. "Go on around and knock."

She was boiling mad, but she didn't want to bite this poor, innocent employee's head off. With a curt nod, she managed a polite smile. "Thanks." Her urge to break every bone in Garth's body was strong, but she couldn't help kneeling to pet Dawg. "Hi there, sweetie." She rubbed his neck, and he took a friendly lick of her arm. "You're looking good. And you smell nice, too."

"Old Dawg don't like this heat, so he stays inside."

She experienced a melancholy tug at her heart, seeing the sweet pooch, and she scratched him between his floppy ears. "I don't blame him." She stood up. "Go on back in, Dawg. I'll see you…" She's almost said "later," but stopped herself. She wouldn't see Old Dawg later. She'd never see him again.

"Well, if that's all, ma'am?"

She nodded, turning away. "Yes—thanks." She'd driven out here with murder in her eye, and she still had to find the man who needed killing. To make matters worse, now her anger was tinged with a crushing sadness.

When she reached Garth's workshop at the far end of the house, she stumbled to a stop. Through a window, she could see him in profile. Practically in the center of a room, he towered over the tools of his trade. Tables and shelves filled with labeled and orderly supplies surrounded him.

He leaned over a saddle that was anchored atop a high-tech sawhorse. In his right hand he used a long, flat knife to scrape and shape the leather seat. Since he wore no shirt, the sun streaming through an abundance of windows highlighted his upper body with bold, golden strokes.

She felt a rending stab in her heart, hating herself for allowing the mere sight of him to hurt her so badly. Making herself turn away, she stalked to the entrance. Too torn up to bother with the formalities of knocking, she threw the door wide. It hit the wall with an explosive report. Cool air engulfed her along with the tang of tanned leather.

He looked toward the door, then straightened and turned in her direction. He was magnificent standing there. Deedee could think of no other word to describe him, with his legs braced wide, his shoulders exquisitely broad, the muscles of his chest and arms hard and distinct in the sunlight.

The beginnings of a smile began to form on his lips, but disappeared at the sight of her obvious rage. He put down his knife, grabbing up his shirt and slipping it on. She watched muscles coil as he moved. With lithe fingers— fingers that had given her intense pleasure—he made quick work of buttoning his shirt. ''It's nice to see you, too,'' he said, eyeing her warily. Tucking in his shirttail, he asked, ''What can I do for you?''

''What can you do for me?'' she echoed, incredulous. Casting around the room, she spied a little hammer and grabbed it. She was startled by how light it was and noticed the head was constructed of some kind of rolled-up material. ''What can you do for me?'' she repeated, her voice an octave higher. ''You can stand still so I can pulverize you. That's what you can do for me!'' She waved the hammer threateningly.

He grimaced. ''You saw the paper?''

She took a menacing step toward him, hammer raised. ''I'm going to murder you!'' She took another step.

He frowned, indicating her weapon. ''Sugar, if you want

to do me in, that rawhide mallet isn't going to get the job done.'' He stepped to a nearby workbench and hefted a larger, lethal-looking tool. ''This is a saddler's hammer.'' He held it out to her, the steel head glinting in the sun. ''It'll kill me dead, if that's what you want.''

She scowled at him. How dare he stand there holding out a hammer for her to kill him with? She ground her teeth. What was going on here? Why didn't he run, or drop to his knees and beg for his life? It was mortifying to discover she couldn't even arouse the emotion of fear in this man.

And why was he pretending to help? She didn't understand him at all.

Her nose started to tickle and her eyes began to sting. With trembling lips, she threw the mallet at him, but he deftly deflected it. ''Why did you do it, Garth?'' she demanded brokenly. ''Why do you hate me so much you had to humiliate me in front of the whole town?''

''Hate you?'' She watched as some elemental emotion deep in his eyes froze the breath in her chest. ''I don't hate you, Dee. I love you.''

She stood like a stump, just staring. This was unquestionably part of his prank, but somehow she couldn't react appropriately. She couldn't take that heavy steel hammer and bash him with it. For some demented reason she stood there longing with every fiber in her being to believe him. Just how stupid could she be?

He lay the hammer aside, moving quickly, silently, taking her hands in his. ''Did you hear me, Dee? I said I love you.''

He spoke so softly she wondered if she was imagining it, wanting it as badly as she did. With a restrained smile he brushed a stray wisp of hair from her troubled face.

"Why would you think my marriage proposal was meant to hurt you?"

Distrustful protests clamored at her lips, but his gaze held hers so gently that she went dumb, physically staggered by the heat in his eyes. Her mouth worked for a few seconds before she could speak. "Well—I—because you propose to every woman you meet! That's why!" Her ire grew with the reminder. He *did* propose to every woman he met. She'd seen him do it a dozen times! Jerking her hands from his grasp, she charged, "I'm not one of your simpleminded bimbettes! And speaking of bimbettes—what about Miss Dice?"

His answer was a low, self-deprecating chuckle. "I didn't have a date with her, if that's what you thought." He shook his head. "Daddy Dice invited me for dinner at his place. When I got there, he asked me to escort Samantha to the store to get steaks to barbecue, and whatever else we wanted."

His smile held a haunting sweetness that touched Deedee's heart in spite of her doubts. "Dice tried to fast-talk me into selling some of my acreage to a developer. And I have a suspicion he'd be happy to marry off his daughter, too." Taking Deedee's hand, he brushed a kiss across her knuckles. "I left at nine. Alone. I drove by your place, but your lights were out." His jaw moved sideways, then clenched. "I sat there in my truck, hoping you'd gone to bed early, but scared to death you were out with some other man."

"I didn't know you knew where I lived," she said, having a hard time taking it all in. Her knuckle tingled where he'd kissed her.

"Of course I knew," he countered softly. "I've driven by a hundred times, wanting to stop. I've picked up the phone a hundred times, too, wanting to hear your voice.

But I never stopped and I never called, because I didn't want to get involved.''

Her heart constricted. She knew that all too well. "What are you saying to me, Garth?"

One big, callused hand cupped her nape and drew her nearer. "Think about it, Dee," he whispered. "I put it in writing this time." His eyes glowed.

The intensity of his gaze was so seductive she felt torn in pieces. She wanted him—she loved him—but could he really have changed? She felt awkward and unsure, and her eyes were suddenly awash with tears. "Don't be cruel to me, Garth," she pleaded.

He took her into his embrace. "You're the cruel one," he murmured, his voice unsteady. "Making me propose in front of God and everybody." He tilted her chin up so that she could see his eyes. They glistened with emotion. "That was cruel," he whispered, his smile tender.

Her head spinning, she pressed her hands to his chest. "But—but you told me not to get serious. You said you didn't make commitments because you'd break them."

"I know." He closed his eyes and inhaled deeply, looking pained. When he opened them again, he kissed the top of her head. "A man grows up, Dee," he murmured into her hair. "When I found myself dry-cleaning my dog and boiling my socks with lemon, I knew my bachelorhood was on its last legs."

His gentle expression was so galvanizing, it sent a quiver through her. "Garth, I—"

"Let me say this, Dee. I need for you to understand," he interrupted, brushing her temple with his lips. "After I left you at my grandparents' house, I tried to get you out of my head, but I couldn't. Everything you said, everything you did came back to me, over and over. I couldn't sleep without seeing you. I couldn't work without seeing you. I was going crazy. What you said about how I loved my dog and my grandparents haunted me." Warm callused hands moved up to hold her face.

"It finally sank in what you were trying to tell me—what I finally understand. That I *can* love deeply. That I *do*. And the fact that my ex-wife left and I didn't go after her wasn't proof that I can't love a woman all my life. It just proved I was meant to find—" His voice broke. "You."

His brown eyes spoke of his suffering and his passion. She could only stare at the awe-inspiring sight, thunderstruck, hardly able to conceive that Garth Gentry had actually proposed marriage to her. A real love-honor-and-cherish marriage. "But, Garth," she protested weakly. "Why didn't you just ask me like any normal man?"

"I tried. When I saw you in that store, I knew I had to have you in my life. So I asked you out. And when you said no, I tried to make a joke, but it still came out a proposal. Remember?" She saw renewed torment flicker in his eyes. "Dee, when you walked away that day, my heart walked away with you." He drew her close, and she felt beautifully crushed by his strength. "I decided I had to do something drastic to get your attention." She felt his heart pounding hard against her own. "Do I have it now?" he asked urgently.

A surge of joy rushed through her. It was really true. Oscar had said Garth was either a damn jackass or he was crazy in love with her. But in her wildest imaginings she had never dreamed…

Suddenly she felt different—stronger and *loved*. The sensation was stimulating, triggering primitive, lusty emotions only Garth could stir in her. His body, lean and hard against hers, made wordless promises she knew he could fulfill. The effect of knowing he was offering her an eternal kind of love spread through her like wildfire, heating her blood. She smiled into his handsome face, joy bubbling up inside her. For the first time in her life, she felt fully alive. "You're not getting serious on me, are you, sugar?" she teased, imitating his lazy drawl.

The grin he flashed was crooked and sheepish. "Kiss me and I'll show you serious."

His smile dimmed suddenly, and his eyes gleamed with such naked vulnerability it stole her heart and her breath. "I'll say it again, Dee. I love you and I want you to be my wife." His vow was warm against her lips. "I can't get more serious than that."

Her smile died, too, for his quiet covenant was too precious to take lightly.

They looked into each other's eyes, communicating as only lovers can. Something undeniable began to build between them, something wonderful. Something that would not—and need not—be denied. Not any longer.

"Do you mind if I take off my glasses?" she murmured at last, her smile meaningful.

His lips quirking, he removed them for her, laying them on a nearby table. "Anything else, boss lady?" His query was low and husky.

She nuzzled his throat. "I want to make love to you, right here, right now."

A playful look came into his eyes. Nudging the door closed with his boot, he lifted her in his arms. "I like a bossy woman in bed."

"But there isn't any bed," she noted, wrapping her arms about his neck.

"Have you ever made love on soft rolls of tanned leather?" he asked.

Laughter gurgled in her throat. "No, I can't say I have."

She wasn't sure she should ask, but she had to. "And you?"

"Not yet." His gaze glittered with flecks of golden sunshine. "But I have a feeling it's going to become a gratifying family tradition."

As he gently set her on a table piled with layers of plush suede, she was dazzled by what she saw in his gaze. Eternity. Pure and unmistakable. This glimpse at the depth of his love was so powerful it made her heart swell almost to bursting. "By the way, Garth—my answer is yes," she murmured. "I will marry you."

He scanned her face, his expression filled with soft devotion. "Just one thing, sugar." He flashed a melting grin before leaning close, his lips covering hers in a white-hot declaration of love.

"What?" she asked with a wanton moan, clinging helplessly to him, adoring his texture, his scent, his fire.

"After we get married—don't kill my dog."

Their laughter mingled as his kisses moved along her jaw to her throat. With tenderness born of a deep and abiding passion, Garth pressed her to her back.

THE FIRST SATURDAY in September was refreshingly cool for that time of year. But why shouldn't everything be perfect? After all, Deedee and Garth were getting married that day.

A simple ceremony was performed in the great room of Garth's home, with Keystone Lake a panoramic backdrop beyond his picture window. Twenty close friends and family attended. Dawg and Magnolia were there, too, cuddled together on a rug. They'd taken to each other so well that Magnolia tagged everywhere after the big, sweet mutt.

The pets were asleep now, with Magnolia snuggling against Dawg in an out-of-the-way corner. Perry and Clara,

Oscar and his wife, along with the other newspaper folks and a mixed bag of well-wishers, chatted and ate cake.

Garth stood before his stone mantel, happier than he had any right to be. He grinned as he watched his new bride make animated conversation with the guitarist who'd provided the wedding music. Deciding it was time to whisk her away to their honeymoon hideaway on the big island of Hawaii, he joined her.

"Dee?" He draped a possessive arm about her shoulders. "What are you doing?"

She looked up, her cheeks pinkened charmingly. "Hi, honey." She indicated the guitar. "I was telling Mike here that if he rubbed down his guitar with toothpaste it'd really glow."

Garth could hardly contain his amusement and lightly kissed her lips. "That's nice." Cocking his head toward his den, he murmured, "Mrs. Assistant Managing Editor, may I have a private word with you?"

Her expression grew curious. He loved the way her brows quirked together. Lord, he adored this woman.

"Sure, honey." She turned toward the guitarist, who was grinning at them both. "Remember, Mike. Toothpaste. Rub it in, then buff it really good."

Mike nodded as Garth took her hand and led her away from the gathering. "What is it?" she asked, once they were alone in the den.

"It's time to leave for our honeymoon." He tugged her into his arms, kissing the tip of her nose. He loved that nose. Lifting her glasses away, he kissed one sweet eyelid and then the other. Those eyes made him weak. They always had. "I can't wait to get you alone," he said, his voice rough with desire. "I've got some rubbing and buffing to do, too."

He watched her eyes grow wide at his sexy promise, her

mouth curved in a smile of feminine anticipation, and he sucked in an appreciative breath. That face was the most beautiful sight he ever hoped to see.

"Really, Garth?" Her pretty blue eyes twinkled. "Rubbing *and* buffing?"

"Yeah," he murmured, his long, hot kiss making promises with his lips, his tongue, his teeth. "And, sugar, when I'm done," he growled seductively, "you're gonna glow."

And darn his sexy hide—the rascal was right.

# LOVE & LAUGHTER

## Marriage Makers

### by Cathie Linz

Once upon a time, three bumbling fairy god-mothers set out to find the Knight triplets their soul mates. But... Jason was too sexy, Ryan was too stubborn and Anastasia was just too smart to settle down.

*But with the perfect match and a little fairy dust...*
*Happily Ever After is just a wish away!*

**March 1998—**
TOO SEXY FOR MARRIAGE (#39)

**June 1998—**
TOO STUBBORN TO MARRY (#45)

**September 1998—**
TOO SMART FOR MARRIAGE (#51)

Available wherever Harlequin books are sold.

Look us up on-line at: http://www.romance.net          HLLMM

# DEBBIE MACOMBER

*invites you to the*

HEART OF TEXAS

Join Debbie Macomber as she brings you the lives and loves of the folks in the ranching community of Promise, Texas.

If you loved Midnight Sons—don't miss Heart of Texas! A brand-new six-book series from Debbie Macomber.

Available in February 1998 at your favorite retail store.

## Heart of Texas by Debbie Macomber

| | |
|---|---|
| Lonesome Cowboy | February '98 |
| Texas Two-Step | March '98 |
| Caroline's Child | April '98 |
| Dr. Texas | May '98 |
| Nell's Cowboy | June '98 |
| Lone Star Baby | July '98 |

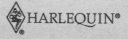
HARLEQUIN®

HPHRT1

*with* Limited Edition **CD**

AN **ALABAMA** BOOK

And listen to Alabama sing their famous song on the free CD enclosed with the book!

*Angels* AMONG US

*A hit song by one of country music's all-time great bands is now the inspiration for a heartwarming new book!*

*Angels Among Us* features stories about people who, through their acts of kindness, have made the world a better place for all of us.

Don't miss your chance to pick up this beautiful hardcover (with special CD enclosed!), just in time for graduation and Mother's Day!

Available in May 1998 at your favorite retail outlet.

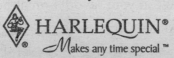

**HARLEQUIN®**

*Makes any time special* ™

PBAMA

# MEN at WORK

**All work and no play? Not these men!**

## April 1998

### *KNIGHT SPARKS* by Mary Lynn Baxter

Sexy lawman Rance Knight made a career of arresting the bad guys. Somehow, though, he thought policewoman Carly Mitchum was framed. Once they'd uncovered the truth, could Rance let Carly go...or would he make a citizen's arrest?

## May 1998

### *HOODWINKED* by Diana Palmer

CEO Jake Edwards donned coveralls and went undercover as a mechanic to find the saboteur in his company. Nothing— or no one—would distract him, not even beautiful secretary Maureen Harris. Jake had to catch the thief—*and* the woman who'd stolen his heart!

## June 1998

### *DEFYING GRAVITY* by Rachel Lee

Tim O'Shaughnessy and his business partner, Liz Pennington, had always been close—but never *this* close. As the danger of their assignment escalated, so did their passion. When the job was over, could they ever go back to business as usual?

## MEN AT WORK™

Available at your favorite retail outlet!

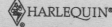 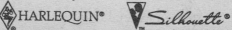

Look us up on-line at: http://www.romance.net          PMAW1

Catch more great
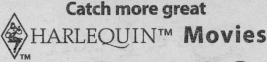
HARLEQUIN™ **Movies**
featured on

## Premiering May 9th
### *The Awakening*

starring Cynthia Geary and
David Beecroft, based on the novel by
Patricia Coughlin

Don't miss next month's movie!
Premiering June 13th
*Diamond Girl*
based on the novel by bestselling author
Diana Palmer

If you are not currently a subscriber to
The Movie Channel, simply call your
local cable or satellite provider for more
details. Call today, and don't miss out
on the romance!

 HARLEQUIN®

*100% pure movies.*
*100% pure fun.*

*Makes any time special* ™

Harlequin, Joey Device, Makes any time special and Superromance are trademarks of
Harlequin Enterprises Limited. The Movie Channel is a service mark of Showtime Networks, Inc.,
a Viacom Company.

An Alliance Television Production

# LOVE & LAUGH

## INTO JUNE!

### #45 TOO STUBBORN TO MARRY
*Marriage Makers*, Book II
Cathie Linz

Three bumbling, fumbling fairy godmothers determine that it's time for Deputy U.S. Marshal Ryan Knight to wed! The only problem is he'd already met Miss Right and had just been too stubborn to marry. Now the busy matchmakers fix it so that Courtney Delaney—the woman who stole Ryan's heart—is his next assignment....

### #46 HOW THE WEST WAS WED
Jule McBride

Sweet-talkin', sweet-kissin' Jackson West has quite a way with the ladies—and a reputation to uphold. So when the sexy cowboy wagers he can seduce Purity, Miracle Mountain's newest celebrity, he quickly learns he's stepped in it. Because the only way into the lady's life is for Jackson to dress up as "Mrs. Simpson," Purity's housekeeper!

### *Chuckles available now:*

### #43 THERE GOES THE BRIDE
Renee Roszel
### #44 THE GREAT ESCAPE
Cheryl Anne Porter

## LOVE & LAUGHTER™

RICHTON PARK PUBLIC LIBRARY DISTRICT

3 6087 00186 5844

*DEC*

*2016*

Victoria Woodhull has done a work for women that none of us could have done. She has faced and dared men to call her the names that make women shudder, while she chucked principle, like medicine, down their throats. She has risked and realized the sort of ignominy that would have paralyzed any of us who have longer been called strong-minded.

Leaping into the brambles that were too high for us to see over them, she broke a path into their close and thorny interstices with a steadfast faith and glorious principle would triumph at last over conspicuous ignominy, although her life might be sacrificed. And when, with a meteor's dash, she sank into a dismal swamp, we could not lift her out of the mire or buoy her through the deadly waters. She will be as famous as she had been infamous, made so by benighted or cowardly men and women... In the annals of emancipation, the name... Victoria Woodhull will have its own place as a deliverer.

—Elizabeth Cady Stanton, 1876, before she and Susan B. Anthony wrote Victoria out of history...

YOU ARE RESPONSIBLE
FOR ANY DAMAGE AT
TIME OF RETURN

# THE RENEGADE
# QUEEN

EVA FLYNN

Ω

OMEGA
PRESS

Ω Omega Press

© 2016 Eva Flynn

**Publisher**: Omega Press
**Author**: Eva Flynn
**Editors**: Amanda L. Boyle, Sam Clapp
Cover design by Alan Clements

ISBN: 978-0-9969832-0-4

All rights reserved. No part of this book may be reproduced in any form or by any electronic or mechanical means, including information storage and retrieval systems—except in the case of brief quotations embodied in critical articles or reviews—without permission from the author at eva@rebellioustimes.com. This book is a work of fiction, based on historical events.
For more information on the author and her works, please see www.rebellioustimes.com.

**Social media connections:**
Twitter: @Evaflyn
Facebook: Eva Flynn_author
Goodreads: Eva Flynn